Calming
the
Storm

Melanie D. Snitker

ISBN: 1500756709
ISBN-13: 978-1500756703

CONTENTS

MELANIE D. SNITKER

In loving memory of my dad,
Robert E. Allison
November 7, 1947 – November 19, 2011
Until we meet again in heaven
I love you

Chapter One

Brandon Barlow looked over the top of the book he was reading. There was a sea of heads bent over desks as they mulled over the small, blue booklets in front of them. The sounds of pens and pencils creating words on paper filled the room as they echoed off the pale yellow walls. All twenty-four of his students worked diligently on their midterm exams for the remaining thirty minutes that were left before the end of class. It seemed like only yesterday that he had been in their place, studying and working hard towards graduation. It didn't seem possible he could be turning twenty-eight next year. Where did the time go?

His eyes settled on one of the women sitting in the back. Unlike the other students in his class who were just out of high school, Rachel Peters was only a couple of years younger than he was. He remembered looking at her birth date on his student list, surprised she was so much older than the others.

Brandon found himself admiring the long, black strands of hair teasing her face. They'd fallen out of the tight ponytail she often wore. He hadn't talked to her much, but it was enough to know she had recently begun taking college courses in her quest to receive a degree in health science. His class was one of the required classes. He also knew she was determined. She worked harder than most of his students normally did, and she wasn't afraid to stand up for something if the class discussions turned to a debate.

He smiled slightly as he remembered her getting into a heated argument with a classmate just last week. Her dark eyes had flashed, and she'd stood her ground as she debated her point. Brandon often wondered what life's adventures had brought her into college later than the typical student. If he were honest with himself, he'd have to admit he thought about her a lot lately. If she wasn't his student, he might have made an attempt to get to know her better outside of the college setting.

Rachel used a slender finger to hook some of her hair behind her ear and stifled a yawn before returning her attention to the blue booklet.

Brandon noted the dark circles under her eyes. For the first exam of the semester, he was concerned about her test results. She hadn't missed a class until the last two. He hoped it wouldn't affect her grade, which up to this point, had been a solid A. Something had recently changed in her life.

Brandon glanced at his watch and then turned his attention back to his book. He nodded at students as they finished ahead of time and handed their tests to him on their way out of the classroom.

At exactly eleven, he stood and cleared his throat. "That's the time. Please bring your papers to the front, and I'll make sure to have these graded and back to you on Friday."

Some of his students looked confident on their way out, and others more nervous. He was certain all were relieved the test was over and they could move forward with the day.

When Rachel left her test, she didn't meet his eyes. Normally one of his friendlier students, the lack of her usual "have a good day" immediately put Brandon on the alert. When he had the room to himself, he picked up her test and flipped through it. With a frown, he put it back on the desk.

She hadn't even finished the last third of the test.

~

Rachel sighed and slung her backpack over her shoulder. She knew she had blown that test and it was going to mess up her GPA. Rachel also knew she'd studied about as much as she possibly could've given the circumstances.

Her thoughts turned to her three-year-old niece who was waiting for her at the campus daycare center. Kendra was beautiful — and a mini image of her mother. Rachel thought about her older sister, Macy. It wasn't fair that Kendra was going to grow up without her mom. "Or that I don't have a sister anymore," she whispered to herself.

It was just a couple of weeks ago that Rachel had gotten the call. She'd been studying in their small apartment, one of her favorite CDs playing loudly in the background. The shrill ring of the phone interrupted the song, and Rachel had to hit the power button on the player quickly so she could answer it. The apartment fell silent. For some reason, the sound of the fridge humming stuck in her mind as she listened to a police officer inform her that Macy and her sister's boyfriend, Ryan, had been killed in a car accident. The roads were exceptionally slippery and their car hydroplaned right off the pavement and into a tree. Their daughter in the back seat had survived uninjured.

As Rachel listened to the officer, she'd collapsed to the kitchen floor, the cold linoleum tiles seeping through the fabric of her jeans like the pain that was engulfing her heart.

The loss was just another chain in a long string of defeats.

Macy had referred to them as life's storms. Their parents had both chosen drugs, and the lifestyle that went with them, over their daughters. As a result, the girls entered the foster care system when Rachel was only five and Macy ten.

If it hadn't been for Macy taking custody of Rachel as soon as she was able to, Rachel would have continued to grow up in the system, floating adrift in a storm that felt like it would never end. Her sister had given her a home and a family. For the first time in her life, things seemed normal.

Rachel should have known better. There might be dry spells, but in life there was always rain on the horizon. Now here she was again, battling a relentless storm and afraid her little lifeboat was going to sink right out from under her. Those virtual waves had battered her all of her life, eating away at her hope until scars had been formed by the erosion. She'd tried her best, and yet here she was again — alone and drifting. Rachel felt tears threatening to fall and she blinked them away. She hadn't cried since she'd been told Macy was dead, and she wasn't going to start now.

"You're not alone," she reminded herself. She had Kendra. Her sweet niece needed her.

~

Brandon helped his younger brother, Trent, load the large buckets of McIntosh apples into the back of the pickup truck. Several leaves came off the stems, floating on the gentle breeze to eventually land unnoticed on the thick grass. They got back into the truck bed and leaned against the sides as their father drove to the next collection of buckets. "Something is going on with her, Trent. I'm really concerned."

Trent shrugged. He looked up at the overcast sky. Rain was in the forecast and it looked like it could start falling any moment now. They were used to working in the rain in northwest Oregon. "What can you do? Mention something to her advisor?"

"Yeah, maybe. Something has happened in the last couple of weeks. I graded her paper last night, and she got a D after getting nothing but A's the whole semester."

The pickup slowed, and the brothers loaded more buckets of the red and green fruit. It was the last stop and they settled down as the truck picked up speed and headed back to the main house. A trail of dust swirled in the air behind them. When the truck rolled to a stop, they jumped over the sides, their boots hitting the packed dirt driveway.

"Thanks, boys." Charles Barlow dusted his gloves off on his pants and then clapped them both on the shoulders. "Always appreciate the help."

"You bet, Dad." Brandon watched as Trent waved at them both and headed for his truck and eventually his own house that was just out of sight on the other side of the property. "Did you need help with the fencing on the north end? Or were you going to do it later?"

"I'll wait on it until this weekend."

Brandon nodded.

"Problems with a student?"

Brandon knew enough of the conversation had probably drifted on the wind for his dad to figure out what was going on. "It's Rachel. You remember me talking about her?"

Charles nodded, waiting patiently for his son to continue.

"She's gone from straight A's to a D on this last test. She didn't even finish the paper. It's not like her. She skipped two classes last week and seems stressed out. I'm concerned about her."

He stopped and turned to look at his dad, who stood a good head taller than himself. Despite the graying hair, there was no doubt that they were father and son. If he'd heard it once he'd heard it a million times — Brandon was the spitting image of Charles Barlow. "I think I may schedule a conference with her even though I'm not her advisor. I wouldn't hesitate to do that if she was one of my other students. But Rachel — well, it's not like she's a kid."

Charles rubbed the stubble on his chin thoughtfully. "I think a conference would probably be a good idea. It can't hurt, and it certainly wouldn't be out of place given the circumstances."

Brandon was relieved to have his plans confirmed. "Meanwhile, if you don't mind, would you and Mom keep her in your prayers?"

"Of course, Brand. Are you heading back to the house?"

"Yeah. I've got some more papers to grade before class tomorrow."

"Alright. Maybe we'll see you at dinner Saturday."

"You bet, Dad. See you later."

Brandon got into his navy blue Toyota Camry and started it up, heading down the dirt road to the opposite end of the large piece of land his family owned. It was a home he had designed and built a couple of years ago. His parents had set aside a section of the land for him and another for Trent. Since Brandon had been saving money for a while, he eventually decided to go ahead and build his home. Living there instead of the apartment in town made it easier to help his dad with the orchard.

Originally, he had planned to rent in town until he married and then have his wife help with the designs. With no real prospects, he decided he might as well have the house built, enjoy it, and live closer to family in the meantime.

Trent was three years younger and had built his house before Brandon even started planning his own. But Trent had to get a head start — he'd proposed to his girlfriend of two years, and they'd recently celebrated their fourth anniversary. He thought about his brother, sister-in-law, and their two-year-old son. He could barely see the top of their house to the east. They were expecting their second child in February, and young Benjamin was excited about being a big brother.

The familiar ache lay heavy in the pit of Brandon's stomach as he exited the car and made his way up the stone path to his front door. The long-standing desire to one day have a family of his own hit hard. To come home to a wife and be welcomed by the sounds of children running through the house was a dream he still held on to.

Instead of a warm kiss and tiny arms giving him a hug, only silence and the welcome blast of cooler air ushered him out of the unusually warm fall weather. Brandon changed into a black shirt and a pair of shorts, settling with a soda at the kitchen table to finish the grading. He found his mind kept drifting to Rachel's face the day before and how tired and defeated she'd looked.

Laying his pen down, Brandon massaged his temples with two of his fingers. "Father, I don't know what's going on in Rachel's life right now. But I feel compelled to pray for her. I ask that You give her comfort, peace, and guidance. If there's some way I can help her, please open the right doors to make that possible. Thank You for all of Your blessings."

~

Friday morning was stressful. Kendra had awakened multiple times during the early hours of the morning thanks to nightmares. They were always a variation of the same dream where either she or her parents became lost and she's unable to find them again. Sometimes it happened in a store, and sometimes it happened in the car while they're driving.

The result was always the same — a little girl with sweat-soaked hair and tears that chase each other down her face. Rachel and her niece slept in the same bed because when they didn't, the nightmares were twice as frequent and the little girl even harder to console.

They were running late. Rachel was already dreading her biology class, and she hadn't had time to grab breakfast for herself — not that the last part was unusual.

Kendra's backpack was ready, containing an extra set of clothes and snacks. Rachel picked it up and called over her shoulder, "Come on, sweetheart, it's time to go."

"I'm coming, Auntie. I have to make sure Candy is ready for her nap."

Rachel didn't have to go into their bedroom to visualize Kendra tucking her toy monkey under a blanket on the bed before giving her a kiss goodbye. She was relieved to see her niece come out, both shoes still on her feet, when the phone rang.

With a frustrated sigh, and a barely contained urge to chuck the phone into the nearby kitchen sink, Rachel turned to pick it up.

"Hello?"

"Is this Rachel Peters?"

"Yes, it is, but I'm on my way out the door for a class."

"This will only take a moment. My name is Morgan, and I'm the apartment complex manager. I understand you are the main occupant of that apartment, is that correct?"

"Yes, I am." Rachel leaned against the counter, dread settling in her stomach like a rock. Kendra stood at her feet, looking up at her curiously. Rachel glanced at her watch and stamped down the intense impatience boiling up inside. They were going to be late again. She tried to focus on the words coming through the phone. She reached up with her free hand to grasp the ends of her ponytail and wrap the strands in circles around her finger.

"I am so sorry for your loss." The woman paused. "I hate to even bring this up, but I didn't know if you were aware that the rent for the apartment is past due by two months."

Rachel was wishing she could go back to bed and start the day over again. Or maybe skip it altogether. "How much money is owed to bring the rental agreement up to date?"

Morgan gave her a number, and Rachel's heart plummeted. "We can give you three weeks to get everything caught up, but that's all we can do." Rachel didn't have anything to say. She stood in silence until Morgan spoke again. "Miss? Are you still there?"

"Yes, I'm here. I have three weeks to come up with that money or we'll need to move out. Do I understand you correctly?"

"I'm so sorry, but yes. We have a long waiting list for these apartments and if you are unable to keep up with the rent, we'll have to ask you to leave in lieu of someone who can."

Rachel could tell by the woman's voice that she wasn't at all enjoying this aspect of her job. She wanted to be upset. Wanted to tell her what she could do with her apartment agreement. But Rachel knew it wouldn't be fair to lash out like that when the woman was just doing her job. "I understand. I'll do what I can and get back to you."

"Wonderful and thank you. Again, I am truly sorry for your loss."

Rachel replaced the phone. There was no way she was going to come up with that kind of money. Looking around her, she was already taking inventory of what she could sell. There wasn't much since the last time she had gone through and parsed out their meager belongings. Between Kendra, classes, and only a part-time campus job, she was drowning in debt as it was, much less if she had to find a new place to live.

It had been rough financially before the accident, but Macy and Ryan had insisted that she stay with them to avoid student housing. They also had paid for her books while she had relied on student loans for the rest. The thought of those student loans made her feel sick now. Especially since there had been no insurance money after the accident.

"Someone in this family needs to get a good education," Macy had told her with a teasing smile. "You can support the rest of us when you become a surgeon and are making millions." The plan had barely worked when there were three of them bringing money into the household. Now that she had a child to support on her own, something needed to be done.

She looked at her watch again and pushed away from the counter. "Okay, Kendra, we've got to get you to school." She held her hand down, waited for the little girl to grasp it with her own, much smaller hand, and led her out the door.

As Rachel drove to daycare, she looked in the rearview mirror. Kendra, with her hair the color of nutmeg and dark green eyes, was like a mini version of Macy. The thought made her throat tighten.

By the time she dropped Kendra off at daycare

with hugs and kisses and then drove to class, she was ten minutes late. She rushed through the door, focusing on her desk at the other end of the room.

As soon as she entered, Professor Barlow paused in his lecture to place Wednesday's exam on her desk. He met her eyes with concern and then went back to his lecture.

Rachel, tuning out his voice, turned the paper over and caught her breath at the large D staring back at her. At the bottom of the paper was a sticky note asking her to speak with him after class.

It was hard to believe that life had been somewhat under control a few short weeks ago.

It's easy, Rachel. You have school to pay for and attend, you have to find a place to live, you have a child to care for, and a full-time job to find. One of them is going to have to give, and I think it's obvious which it has to be.

Getting a degree in the health sciences wasn't exactly something she had dreamed of as a child. She had always hoped to marry, have children, and be the kind of mom who was there during the day — at least until her kids were of school age. But real life had a way of creeping into any dream. At least the medical field was one that was useful and her skills would be in demand. She knew she could find a job if she could get through this and graduate.

Who was she kidding? She needed to find whatever job she could in order to pay the bills and be home in the evenings with Kendra. Right now, the daycare costs alone were killing her financially. She knew the last of the meager savings in the bank had disappeared and how she was going to pay the next daycare bill was beyond her.

Frustrated and feeling overwhelmed, she clenched

her fist. Why couldn't she get a break? She was sick and tired of having no control over her life, no power over anything that happened to her. Right now, it felt like the water pouring through the cracks in her life was getting deeper. She knew she wasn't far from drowning, and it was time to do what she needed to in order to survive.

Rachel truthfully couldn't have told anyone what the day's lecture was about. She waited until everyone else had made their way out of the room before approaching her instructor. She held her paper out to him. "I don't even know what to say."

Brandon took it from her. "This is very unlike you, Rachel. Is something going on?"

She shrugged, looking down at an invisible spot on the floor near her right shoe. "This isn't an easy class."

"You're right about that; it's not an easy class. Despite that, you've managed to keep up with the lecture, and you've done well on the tests." Professor Barlow held the most recent booklet up. He tapped it with a finger. "Until this one. I know you're capable of doing better than this."

Rachel's dark eyes flashed, and her chin raised a bit as she said firmly, "You don't know me or what I'm like. Do you want an apology for the bad grade? Trust me, I'm sorry. I can't express how sorry I am. But don't even try to tell me what I am or am not capable of."

Chapter Two

The force of her words caught Brandon off guard. He watched as some of the hair from her ponytail slid forward to hide part of her face, though it didn't come close to masking the determination that radiated from her every pore. He resisted the urge to sweep the hair to the side so that he could see her eyes better.

"Look, I don't want an apology here. You've done an amazing job this semester. I hate to see you mess up your grade like this now." He handed the test back to her. "I would like to schedule a conference with you, talk about this, and see if maybe we can set up some extra study sessions. I'm sure some of the other students could use them as well. This section of the class is especially complex."

Rachel immediately shook her head. "That won't be necessary. I'll be bringing by a form to drop the class on Monday." She turned to leave, but Brandon instinctively reached for her arm to stop her. When she turned to face him again he released her, though he was aware of how soft her skin had been under his hand.

"Why would you want to drop the class? This is one grade — one test. It's not the end of the world." Brandon couldn't help but take the possibility of her dropping his class as anything but personal.

"It's only the one test in this class," she said quietly. Her stomach chose then to rumble loud enough that Brandon could hear it clearly. He noticed, for the first time, that her face looked pale in contrast to her dark hair. A slight pink dusted her cheeks when she realized he'd heard her body's admission of hunger. She wrapped her arms around her middle as if that could put an end to her need for food.

"I don't have anything going on now. Why don't you join me in the cafeteria? We'll get some lunch and maybe we can figure this out."

Rachel looked hesitant, and he was afraid she was going to turn him down. *Please, God, there has to be something I can do.*

"You have to eat," he reminded her, and almost on cue her stomach let loose another rumble.

Rachel's blush spread to her ears. Just when Brandon was sure she would say no, she agreed. With a little nod, she shouldered her backpack and waited for him to lead the way.

They walked silently to the cafeteria where they both filled their trays and then chose a corner table where it was easier to talk. When they had taken a seat, Brandon gave her a long look. "So what's going on?"

Rachel shrugged and took a bite of her spaghetti, moving the plate so that it was exactly between them like some kind of shield. Brandon was glad she at least chose something of substance to eat. He waited patiently while she chewed and took a drink. She finally looked up at him, and his heart clenched at the sadness that swam in her brown eyes.

"Rachel, you seem to have a lot going on. You have to talk to someone."

Brandon was surprised at how quickly the sadness in her eyes was replaced by irritation. "Why should you be that person?"

He didn't say anything for a few moments as he took a drink of his soda and watched the woman in front of him take another bite of her lunch. Even now, when she was clearly stressed and tired, she looked beautiful. He caught himself, for the second time that day, wishing he could brush some of that hair away from her face and sweep some of the cares in her world with it. Brandon surprised himself with the realization, but was unwilling to examine that too closely right now.

Rachel finished her lunch — or at least all she was going to eat of it — and sat back in her chair. She watched him for a moment before beginning. "It's not just your class. I'm dropping all of my classes this week."

"Why? You're a focused student. You have a lot to offer the medical field."

"I don't have time for that anymore. It's the second week of October and there's only another week-and-a-half before it's too late to drop classes as it is." She picked up her napkin and began to twist it in her hands. "Several things have come up that will not allow me to continue with my studies. I truly no longer have the time for them, or the money to pay for classes."

"There has to be something else you can do." Brandon felt she was one of the most gifted students he'd taught, even if she did lack some of the passion for the medical field that he might have expected. The thought of Rachel not getting the education she deserved bothered him. His eyes followed her hands, fingers long and delicate, as they worried the napkin until bits of the paper were dusting the table below it.

Rachel scrutinized him, clearly trying to reach a decision. "There's nothing anyone can do." She tossed the mangled napkin onto her half-empty plate and stood quickly. "I really do need to go. I have a lot of paperwork to get in order." She stood, thanked him for the meal, and began to walk out of the cafeteria.

In an attempt to catch up, Brandon rushed to slide the trays together, grabbed his bag, and jogged after her. "Rachel! Wait up a minute, please."

She slowed, but didn't turn. "Look, Professor Barlow, I appreciate your concern. But I've gone through a lot of my life on my own and I've managed to make it so far. I'll be bringing that form by on Monday." That said, she resumed her escape. Brandon could only watch her go, her words replaying in his mind. He wished he could have some glimpse into her life, to know what had happened to change her world so much in such a short amount of time.

"God, I don't know what's going on but please give her some of Your peace," he whispered as he watched her disappear.

~

Rachel helped Kendra sit up a little straighter on one of the two chairs in the kitchen. She watched as the girl used a spoon to scoop macaroni out of a bowl. Rachel shook her sippy cup to make sure there was enough milk and then sat down to her own bowl of macaroni. "Did you have fun at school?"

Kendra nodded, a noodle dropping out of her mouth as she tried to chew faster. When she had swallowed, she pointed to her shirt. "Yes! We used finger paint. I almost messed my shirt with the red."

"That sounds like fun! What did you paint?"

"A rainbow with birds and grass and trees and worms. Pink and purple are my favorite, you know."

Rachel chuckled. "Yes, I know. Those are great colors." Pink and purple had been Kendra's favorite colors since she'd been old enough to have a preference. She watched as her niece continued her meal.

Looking around the room, Rachel's gaze fell on the stack of papers on the other side of the table. She had her paperwork ready for all of her classes and would drop them on Monday. She'd changed Kendra's arrangement at daycare from full days, five days a week, to mornings only Tuesdays and Thursdays while she was at her job in the mail center. She wasn't even sure she would still be eligible for the job once she dropped her classes. That would remain to be seen. At least the daycare costs would be drastically reduced. She could always increase the hours again once she found full-time employment.

Rachel glanced at the plain calendar that hung from an orange thumbtack on the wall. There was a meeting with Child Protective Service on Tuesday. It was a meeting she'd refused to think about but it'd been there in the back of her mind since it was first scheduled. She dreamed about the outcome of this particular meeting nearly every night, and the ending was never a happy one. She dreaded the very idea of what the meeting might lead to. *What if they try to take her away from me?*

Rachel kissed the top of Kendra's head and laid her cheek against the warm, silky hair. There was only one thing that made sense in her world right now — and Rachel clung to her like she was the last thing keeping her afloat as she battled this particular storm in her life.

~

Monday morning dawned bright, promising another humid day ahead. It had rained over the weekend and that in combination with the unusually warm weather they were experiencing resulted in air that was exceptionally sticky. Brandon awoke with Rachel on his mind, and he hoped to get to class to discover his student had found a solution to her troubles — one that did not include dropping his class. He was disappointed when Rachel didn't show up until the very end of class. Nearly all of the students had left when she walked in, a piece of paper in one hand. A small girl clung to her other hand as she looked curiously around the classroom.

"Hi, Professor Barlow. Here's that drop slip if you wouldn't mind signing it for me."

"Of course." Seeing the girl had caught Brandon completely by surprise, and he had to work to school his features. He took the slip from her and numbly signed his name to it, handing it back again just as quickly. Double-checking her left hand, he confirmed that there was no wedding ring. He was sure he would have noticed one before. He briefly wondered why it mattered then tried not to focus on how relieved he was to find she wasn't married. Her words brought his attention from her left hand to her eyes.

"Look, I appreciate you trying to help. It's more than anyone else has done for me in a long time. I know I've been abrupt, and I didn't want to leave without apologizing about that." Rachel's dark eyes studied him, pleading for him to understand.

Brandon frowned. How sad that his futile attempts to get her to stay in college had ranked so high on the list of efforts anyone had put into her life. He found himself, not for the first time, wishing he knew more about this woman who was standing before him. "Where are you off to next?"

"I have a few more classes to take care of and some financial matters."

"Have you eaten lunch yet?"

Rachel seemed surprised by his question. "No, we haven't."

"When was the last time you ate somewhere decent — no cafeteria food?"

Rachel thought for a moment. "I'm not even sure." Heat rose to her cheeks, and she looked at the girl who gazed back up at her with emerald eyes.

"I'm hungry," she said simply.

Brandon beamed down at her, making a mental note of how much she was paying attention to their conversation. "Then let me take you ladies to get something good for lunch. It won't take that long out of your day. Please." He couldn't deny a basic attraction to Rachel. His head warned him to keep his distance because it was all way too complicated. His heart, however, wasn't going to let him walk away so easily.

"Okay, Professor Barlow. I appreciate that."

With those words, the sense of relief that washed over him told him that he that had done the right thing.

Brandon could feel his heart race as he gathered his things quickly and put them into his messenger bag. "It's Brandon. I'm not your teacher anymore, remember?"

Rachel shrugged. "I won't promise to remember to call you that. Old habits and all."

He followed Rachel to the parking lot and her car. She motioned for him to get in. "Where are we heading?" she asked as she buckled the little girl into her car seat in the back.

"Do you like Mexican food?" She nodded. "I know a great place, then."

~

Following Brandon's directions, Rachel drove them to a local Mexican food restaurant. By the time she'd parked, her stomach was growling. She realized she hadn't eaten breakfast, which led to another startling thought — she couldn't remember the last time she had. She really did need to start paying more attention. What kind of example was this setting for Kendra?

Rachel opened the back door and helped Kendra unbuckle her seat belt. "You ready to get something to eat?"

Kendra looked at Brandon through the window

shyly and nodded. "Yes," she said with a whisper. "I want to sit next to you."

"Of course, sweetheart." She lifted Kendra into her arms and patted her back as she shut the car door.

Rachel could feel Brandon's eyes on them as she lowered Kendra to her feet and slung her bag over one shoulder.

Once inside, they were seated and Rachel scooted Kendra's chair closer to hers.

Rachel watched as Brandon observed them for a moment. "She's beautiful," Brandon said quietly. "How old is she?"

"Just over three-years-old." Rachel looked over to see Kendra cupping her hands around a glass of ice water as she took swigs out of the straw.

"I have a two-year-old nephew." He continued to watch Kendra, giving her a little wave when she looked at him and then smiling when she returned the gesture from behind the glass. "Kids are so much fun. Though at least, in my nephew's case, the energy never ends."

As she watched Brandon ask Kendra a question about her water, Rachel found herself really noticing him for the first time. Sure, she had observed him as he lectured in class and had talked to him plenty of times on her way out. Only now did she realize how much red was in his dark blond hair and that it was just long enough to curl slightly at the nape of his neck above his shirt collar.

The next thing that drew her attention were his eyes. They were green with a hint of brown flecked randomly throughout. It was while she was studying them that he shifted his gaze from Kendra to her, catching Rachel off guard. She felt her face flush as she quickly looked at the menu laid out on the table in front of her. "Everything looks good. It's hard to decide."

Brandon agreed with her and they spent a few moments with their menus until the waiter came to drop off chips and bowls of salsa before taking their orders.

Rachel scooped some salsa onto a chip, took a bite, and was impressed by the taste. They had combined the right amount of cilantro and garlic to make a delicious dip.

Kendra tentatively nibbled on a chip of her own. "Mmmmm. These are good," she said softly, reaching for a second one.

Brandon smiled at Kendra and nodded in her direction. "Your daughter speaks well."

"She does," Rachel agreed, a lump forming in her throat. After all the girl had been through, it continued to amaze Rachel daily how innocently happy she was. "Kendra is my niece, Professor Barlow."

His surprise was evident, and there was something else that flashed in his eyes, disappearing before she had time to decipher its meaning.

"It's Brandon," he reminded her quietly. His mouth opened again, as though he was going to ask her a question, but he thought better of it. Instead, he seemed to focus on his chips and salsa for a time.

"You said you have a nephew. Do you have any children?"

He shook his head. "No. But I do live very near my brother and his family so I'm around my nephew regularly."

"That must be nice," she said with a smile, though

the thought that her sister would miss all of those changes, all of those years watching her daughter grow, filled her with sadness. She had to avert her eyes in an attempt to blink away the sheen. *Keep it under control, Rachel.* She didn't have time for this. She had other, more important things to focus on, namely the little girl reaching for another drink. "Here, let me get that closer to you. Do you want to try the salsa?"

Kendra shook her head, and after finishing her drink, said, "No, thank you."

Rachel smiled at her, brushed some hair out of her face, and then turned her attention back to Brandon. "Thanks for suggesting this. The chips and salsa alone are better than anything they have in the cafeteria."

Brandon surprised her by quietly saying, "Would I be right in assuming you skip a lot of meals?"

Rachel hesitated and then shrugged. "Life's busy." What else could she say? It was the truth. The fact that she was low on money and sometimes ate nothing but ramen noodles and saltines wasn't something she was about to mention.

Their food arrived then, and the smell of her chicken enchiladas made her mouth water. She asked the waiter for a second plate. When she cut into the enchiladas, the food steamed. She scooped some of them along with the rice to the little plate for Kendra and then took a bite of them herself. She savored the taste. Rachel then blew on Kendra's food in an attempt to cool it down. She cut the enchiladas up into small pieces and handed the spoon to her niece.

They ate in comfortable silence for a few minutes, Rachel alternating between eating some of her food and helping Kendra when she needed it.

"Rachel, I wish you felt comfortable enough to

tell me what's going on."

She wasn't sure if it was the tone of Brandon's voice or the understanding, encouraging look in his eyes. Or maybe she was just sleepy after one of the first real meals she'd eaten in way too long. While everything inside Rachel screamed at her to stay quiet, to keep it all to herself, there was something about the man sitting across from her that allowed the words to escape her lips. "My sister and her boyfriend were killed in a car accident nearly three weeks ago."

~

"Oh Rachel, I'm so sorry." Brandon's mouth went dry and he cleared his throat. He couldn't even imagine the feelings of loss she had to be going through right now. "Was Kendra ..."

Rachel nodded. "Thank goodness she wasn't hurt. The police said it was a miracle." She smiled softly at the girl who had a ring of enchilada sauce around her lips. "She looks a lot like Macy."

"Your sister?"

"Yeah. Macy was five years older than me."

"There's no other family that can help you?" Brandon was pretty sure he already knew the answer to that question. The woman sitting in front of him wouldn't look so tired and stressed if she had any assistance at all.

Rachel's dark hair shined under the light hanging over the table. "Our parents relinquished us to the state when I was five and we were put into the foster care system. When Macy graduated out of the system, she worked hard to get custody of me and brought me to live with her. Macy was the only family I've ever had. And now I'm that to Kendra." She fell silent, staring thoughtfully at the carbonation bubbles moving through the drink in her glass.

Brandon felt his heart ache for this woman sitting in front of him. He'd always felt blessed to have had the kind of carefree childhood that he experienced. Hearing Rachel's story made him feel even more so. "Are you dropping classes because you don't have the time? Maybe you can get an extension on them. There are school counselors you can talk to. I know one person I can introduce you to ..."

Rachel sat up straighter and cut him off. "I won't be coming back. I can't afford to. I'm losing the apartment we have due to financial difficulty, I certainly can't pay for my classes now, and my guardianship of Kendra is being questioned by the CPS." She shot him a challenging look. "Tell me one of the school counselors can fix that, and I'm all over it."

Brandon blinked at her. "What are you going to do?"

"I honestly don't know. But no matter what, Kendra and I have to stick together." Rachel swallowed hard, fingering the ends of her niece's hair. "Look, Professor Barlow, I'm sorry to drop all this on you. I can't believe I poured out my life story like that."

Brandon ignored her formal use of his name and observed the woman sitting before him. He found himself feeling a great deal of respect for her. She had faced more in life than he could imagine. Now she had a child to care for and yet she was still willing to fight.

"Maybe you needed to talk everything out.

Everyone needs someone to talk to." Rachel shrugged. "You mentioned your guardianship of Kendra was being challenged. What's going on there?"

Rachel frowned and set the glass back down on the table. He didn't think she had actually taken a drink. "I'll know more after a meeting tomorrow. But her dad's aunt and uncle are trying to get custody of her. They are established, have a home, but she's not doing well health-wise. Still, they are a whole lot better off than I am at the moment, and I may have to put up a fight." The fear was evident in her eyes.

Brandon studied her. "Some of that may be true, but you're still this girl's aunt. She's your only blood relative. You're young and more able to raise a small child than they would be. That has to count for something."

She nodded. "I hope so." Rachel paused, regarding him thoughtfully. "I seriously don't know why I'm telling you all of this. It's not any concern of yours and the last thing you need is some crazy lady who has more issues than Swiss cheese has holes taking up your time." She sat up straighter, put her napkin on her plate, and moved to help Kendra with the few bites she had left on her own.

Brandon wanted to object, to say something to prove that he wanted to help. Instead, he followed suit and went to pay their bill. Rachel drove him back to the college so that he could get his own vehicle. As he stepped out of the car, he couldn't shake the feeling that if he didn't do something, he might not see her again after today. Unwilling to examine that whole mess too closely, he acted on instinct. "Why don't I go with you to that meeting? At least I can be a character witness for you."

Brandon truly thought she would dismiss the offer completely, or at least would require some convincing. He was surprised when she quickly agreed.

"It's actually at my apartment. Tomorrow at four in the afternoon."

Brandon nodded his acknowledgement. "I'll be there.

~

Brandon was sitting at his parents' dinner table as the talk of the day floated like falling leaves swirling in the wind. Young Benjamin, his nephew, was sitting between Trent and Melinda talking away in between bites of his French fries. Brandon couldn't help but smile at him as words somehow managed to find their way through the over-filled chipmunk cheeks. Melinda kept going back and forth between answering Benjamin's unending questions to talking to Sarah, Brandon's mom.

Brandon's thoughts drifted to Rachel and it was sobering to realize that she and Kendra ate most meals alone. When Rachel wasn't skipping them.

"Why so serious, Brand?" Charles' question jerked Brandon back to the present. Everyone had turned to look at him.

He forced a smile and tried to dodge the question. "Sorry, it's all good. Just distracted tonight." It was clear no one was going to be redirected, and he couldn't really blame them.

"Mmmhmmm. Nice try, big brother," Trent said from his seat across the table.

Sarah cleared her throat. "Why don't we continue to enjoy this meal?" It was a light-hearted comment, but her family knew that meant a change of topic was in order and they quickly obliged.

When dinner was over, Brandon ventured into the kitchen in search of the cookies he knew were waiting. He lifted the plastic wrap off the plate on the counter, choosing a chocolate chip cookie and polishing it off in one bite.

Footsteps brought his attention to the kitchen door. "Hey, Mom. Great cookies as always." He took another one, putting it in his mouth with a flourish. "I may sneak these home with me when I leave," he said with a wink.

Sarah smiled and teased him by moving the plate away from him and closer to the sink. "I don't think your dad would be too happy about that."

They both laughed at the thought. Charles was well known in the family for his love of cookies of any kind, but especially chocolate chip. A plate of warm cookies was about the best way to butter the guy up if you wanted to ask him something.

"Are you nervous about the meeting tomorrow?"

Brandon had told his parents about Rachel's CPS appointment. "A little. I'm not real sure what to expect or if I can even help her."

"Are you developing feelings for Rachel?"

Leave it to his mom to get right to the point. Even knowing that about her, he hadn't seen this question coming. His face must have revealed his confusion because she squeezed his upper arm and leaned against the counter with him. "There seems to be more going on here than just trying to help a student out of a tough situation."

MELANIE D. SNITKER

Brandon rubbed the stubble that was developing on his chin and blowing out a puff of air. "I barely know her. I feel like I need to help her. I'm not sure where that urgency is coming from, but I do know that I've felt led to pray for her a lot."

Sarah placed a soft hand over his large, tanned one. "Brand, I want you to be careful. This poor girl clearly needs help and she needs a friend. I think it's wonderful that you want to help her — I'm so proud that we've raised you to be the kind of man that would."

Brandon raised an eyebrow. "I sense a 'but' in there somewhere."

Sarah leaned toward him. "It's not an easy situation and there are a lot of complications. The problems she has are more than something you can solve in a week or even a month. I don't want you to get dragged into something that's more than you can handle."

He gave her an understanding smile and kissed her on the cheek. "I'll be careful, Mom. I'm praying, trust me. I do know, without a doubt, that I'm supposed to help her somehow." He ran his fingers through his hair, pausing at the back of his neck. "As for how I feel about her personally, I'm still sorting that out."

"Fair enough. Know that your dad and I are going to be praying for you. And praying for Rachel. Of course, she and her niece are more than welcome to come over for dinner anytime. You know that."

"Thanks, Mom." He straightened as she did and they exchanged a hug. Sarah let her hand linger on his face and then went back out to where everyone else was visiting.

What is going on, Lord? Am I here to help Rachel? Please

36

let there be something I can do to help her keep Kendra. I feel drawn to her and I don't think it's just attraction. I think you put her in my life — or me in hers — for a reason. Please show me that reason and help me to be the friend she needs right now.

~

It was just after three-thirty when Brandon knocked on the door. Rachel opened it quickly, a bunch of towels clutched under one arm. "Hi. Come on in."

Brandon stepped inside, pausing to take in the meager contents of the small apartment. There was a laundry basket on the couch filled with clothes, and he could look through the doorway to see the dishes in the kitchen sink. "Rough day?" He couldn't help but notice that her hair hung loose around her shoulders and how it seemed to glisten under the light from the windows.

Rachel blew some of the long strands out of her face and sighed. "Yeah. And they'll be here in twenty-five minutes. I had to run to the store and that took forever and then we had issues getting the laundry done. Well, let's just say this hasn't been the best afternoon on record."

Brandon held his arms out for the towels. "If you'll tell me where you want these, I'll put them away and then help you with the kitchen."

She hesitated, casting a doubtful look his way. At that point, Kendra walked in, a toy monkey in her arms. Brandon turned his attention to her. "Hi, Kendra. Who have you got there?"

Kendra looked at her aunt first before she looked

back at him and answered, "Her name is Candy. She's my monkey." She held the toy at arm's length towards him. It was clearly a well-loved toy as the brown fur was not as soft as it likely was when it first came from the store. The ribbon on top of the monkey's head had tattered ends. But the girl held the toy in her hands like it was her most treasured possession. "See, she has a purple bow in her hair."

Brandon smiled at her. "So she does. She's a very pretty monkey."

"Thank you," she replied politely. "Auntie? Can I have a towel for Candy? She's sleepy and she needs a blanket to stay warm for her nap."

Brandon watched as Rachel chose a colorful towel and handed it down to her. "Make sure you get her tucked in good so that she can sleep well."

"I will!" Kendra smiled brightly then left the room to what Brandon assumed was a bedroom.

He chuckled. "She's a character."

Rachel afforded him a smile. "Yes, she is." She nodded to the kitchen. "I've got these, but I'm not going to say no to help in the kitchen."

Feeling as though he'd made some kind of progress with Rachel, Brandon got right to work on the dishes. He had them washed quickly and was drying his hands on a towel by the sink when Rachel entered the kitchen.

Dressed in a pair of slacks and a dark purple blouse, Rachel was fussing with her hair. She had left it down and was all but attacking it with a brush. As she worked on her hair with one hand, she shuffled through a stack of papers on the kitchen table with the other. Brandon couldn't tear his gaze away from this woman who clearly could turn multitasking into a career. The black waterfall she was brushing became shiny in response to the strokes and cascaded down her back. He found himself wondering if it felt as smooth and silky as it looked.

"I appreciate the help."

"No problem at all." Brandon shifted his attention from Rachel and sat the towel back down on the counter. "You look really nice."

The lightest shade of pink dusted her cheeks and she dipped her chin quickly. "Thanks. I appreciate you coming to be a character witness. I have no idea if that's even something that they will want, but I have a strong feeling I'm on the losing end of this battle." Rachel glanced at the door leading to the other room and lowered her voice. "I can't lose the only family I have, and I'll take any help I can get today."

Brandon studied her eyes. Vulnerability was replaced so quickly with determination that he might have imagined the first emotion.

There was a knock on the door and Rachel jumped. With a flick of her wrist, she flung her brush through another open door, the clatter of it hitting the floor echoing back out to them. "Let's get this over with," she said.

He waited for Rachel to escort the two women in and offered them a seat on the couch. He brought in one of the two metal kitchen chairs for Rachel to sit on. Kendra came into the living room again, closing the bedroom door behind her. As soon as she saw the newcomers, she ran to Rachel and climbed into her lap.

"I'm Mary O'Dell," the older of the two women introduced herself. "And this is Kathy Miller. We're both from CPS." She paused long enough for Rachel to introduce Brandon before going on to explain the details of CPS, what all they were there for, and how Kendra's great aunt and uncle had expressed a concern for Kendra and was interested in gaining custody of her.

"So what does that mean for me? Are we talking a custody battle?"

"If they continue to pursue this and you do as well, then yes. Right now, you've got temporary guardianship of Kendra and until a court says differently, that will remain. But unless one side or the other relinquishes their claim to her, it will result in a custody battle in court."

Rachel swallowed hard. "What kind of a chance do I have of winning custody?"

Mary and Kathy exchanged looks. It was Kathy's turn to speak.

"You are more than welcome to get a lawyer and pursue this. But it's only fair to let you know that it's going to be difficult for you to win custody."

Brandon sensed Rachel stiffen at the response. "Why?"

"Because the Lawrences have health insurance, he has a full-time job, they own their home, and are very stable." Kathy cleared her throat. "At the moment, you are trying to find a permanent place to live. You have no full-time job, no health insurance."

"Mrs. Lawrence has a lot of health issues. I'm more capable of taking care of Kendra — of raising her." Rachel fought to maintain her composure. Brandon could see the look of defeat spread across her features as her shoulders noticeably slumped. She cradled Kendra protectively in her arms, kissing her cheek.

"Unfortunately, health insurance and money go a long way when it comes to the court system. The relationship to the child is a bit removed for both sets of people involved. There was no will left by her parents expressing who they wanted the child to live with in the event of their passing. It will depend on who can care for the child in the best way."

"The child?" Rachel stood up, frustrated. Kendra wrapped her arms around her aunt's neck. "Her name is Kendra. And she is literally the only living relative I have in this world. My sister and I were close — we were best friends. I know that if Macy and Ryan could say so right now, they would both agree that I would be the best person to raise my niece."

Kathy shuffled papers in her lap. "I'm sorry. Stability and the money to pay for care for the child is a big considering factor when it comes to the judge's decision."

Rachel closed her eyes momentarily, resting her forehead against Kendra's.

It was all Brandon's heart could take. He stood and cleared his throat. "Doesn't a fiancé count for anything?" he asked.

Chapter Three

Rachel's head snapped up and she looked at Brandon. Surely she had heard him wrong. Maybe she should have specified that he show up as her witness void of any excessive alcohol consumption.

Kathy turned to him, really looking at him for the first time since her arrival. "Excuse me? Are you two engaged?"

He took a step forward and Rachel felt him place a hand on her shoulder. "Brandon Barlow. Yes, we're engaged. I've got a full-time job teaching at the college down the street. Both Rachel and Kendra will have full health and dental insurance coverage as soon as we're married."

Not knowing what else to do, Rachel smoothed Kendra's hair away from her face and shifted her to the other hip.

Kathy looked stunned but recovered quickly. "Well, that could definitely make a difference. Although the fact that you are engaged still means the child is not covered by health insurance at this point. We'll need some information about the revenue coming into the household." She jotted a few remarks down on her note pad. "At this point, it looks like we've got about three or four weeks until the first hearing. We'll see what the judge is thinking and go from there."

"How many hearings are we looking at?" Rachel asked.

"It could be settled in the one. Or it could take several. It's hard to say."

Kathy and Mary began packing their things and stood up. "We'll call you when we get the date and time set. Meanwhile, if you have any questions, don't hesitate to contact us." Rachel took the business cards they extended.

They said their goodbyes, and Rachel escorted them out of the house, shutting the door behind them. She turned slowly, throwing Brandon a wary look. "What was that about?"

Brandon slipped his hands into the front pockets of his jeans. "I wanted to test them, make sure this wasn't all just a series of scare tactics to get you to drop the case before the court hearing. We may not agree with making the decision based on income and insurance, but I suppose they have to have a line to draw without getting emotionally involved." He met her gaze, unflinching. "Look, I'm sorry I overstepped my bounds."

"Overstepped your bounds? You truly do have a Clark Kent complex, don't you?"

Brandon tipped his head back, laughing loudly. Kendra started, looking at him with big eyes. He tapped the girl gently on the tip of her nose, still chuckling. "I'll have to tell my brother that, he'll get a good laugh out of it."

Rachel couldn't help but return his smile. "Well, it fits. You seem determined to help someone who doesn't want — or need — your help." She tickled Kendra under the chin and got a smile in return before setting her back down. "The look they gave you was worth it, though."

Brandon's expression sobered. He took a few steps towards her, capturing her eyes with his own. "I totally get that you don't want any help. But you can't look me in the eye and honestly tell me that you don't *need* the help."

Unwilling to respond to his challenge, Rachel held up her right hand. "I'm serious when I say I would consider running."

Brandon blinked at her in surprise. "Run? Where? How would that accomplish anything?"

"They wouldn't be able to find us and separate us." Rachel looked at him pointedly. She knew it probably sounded desperate, but it was the last resort. If it came to it, she would take Kendra and disappear in a heartbeat if it meant not losing her.

"There's got to be something else we can do."

"We?" Rachel laughed, but there was no humor in the sound. He tried to reach a hand out to her arm, but she backed away from his touch. "There's only me. I'm the one to get us out of this mess and do what my sister would want me to do. I've had to rely on myself for the majority of my life, and I can do this on my own, too." She motioned to the door. "I'm thankful that you came here today and for all of your help. But at this point, maybe the less you know the better."

Brandon opened his mouth to say something, but after a long moment, he closed it again. He took a card out of his wallet, used a pen to write down his cell number, and handed it to her. "If you need anything, call me." When she wouldn't look at him, he used an index finger to gently lift her chin until her eyes met his. "Call me."

With that, he took his leave, closing the door behind him.

Rachel sank onto the couch. She could feel a migraine starting. She closed her eyes and rubbed her temple. Brandon's concerned face came to her mind. It was as though his green eyes could see into her heart, and that made Rachel feel uncomfortable. She had lived her life doing everything she could to not appear vulnerable. Somehow, after years of keeping that barrier intact, Brandon had seen right through it in moments.

"Are you okay, Auntie? Does your head have an ouchie?" Kendra gently touched her forehead and the look of concern on her face melted Rachel's heart.

"A little bit, Pumpkin. But I'm fine."

"It'll get better!"

"Yes, it'll get better."

~

Brandon was walking down a row of apple trees. A large number of apples had already been harvested while still more were ripening. The crop this year had been even better than they expected. Their family was blessed. He heard footsteps and turned to see Charles approaching. "Hey, Dad."

"Heya, son. Everything look good?" Charles motioned to the trees around them.

"We've already pulled in a lot of apples, and I

think it's going to get better as the month goes on." Brandon turned to face his father and leaned against a tree. "Can I talk to you for a minute?"

Charles joined his son. "You know you can." He waited in silence as Brandon tried to organize the thoughts that were bouncing around his head like a bunch of rubber balls.

Brandon sighed, running his hand through his hair in frustration. "I've been praying for guidance and direction all week and I'm feeling just as confused as I was when I started."

"What exactly are you confused about? Maybe if you can talk it out, it will help."

"Rachel." Brandon felt his heart quicken as he said her name.

"Are you in love with her?"

Brandon blew out a frustrated breath of air and straightened quickly. "You and Mom must be talking," he said with a laugh. "I just know I feel really protective of her. I think it's because she's fighting an uphill battle and doesn't have a single person on her side. It doesn't seem right." He leaned back against the tree. "The fact is, all I can think of is that if it were Melinda or Mom or even Trent, I would want someone to try to help them through a difficult time. If my life had been different, if I were in her position and all I had in the world was Benjamin, I would do anything in my power to keep him with me."

Charles shifted his weight and put a hand on his son's shoulder. "Brand, you're loyal to your family — almost to a fault. You should be off teaching at Harvard or someplace like that instead of sticking so close to help your old man." Brandon gave him a feigned looked of annoyance. Charles responded with a playful push. "Rachel would be lucky to have you in her corner."

"So you think I should try to help her?"

"If that's how you feel God leading you, then yes."

Brandon nodded thoughtfully. "I'm worried she's going to take Kendra and run. I suspect she's worse off financially than she lets on. She's skipping meals, and I doubt it's because she's too busy to eat. If she runs, I can't imagine she's going to be able to do much better. They will have a warrant out on her for kidnapping. How is she going to get a job to support them like that? Will they live in her car?"

"It's not an easy situation, that's for sure," Charles agreed.

"Dad, she has no money, no insurance. No chance to keep that little girl." He paused and looked at Charles, an idea suddenly forming in his head. "I have a steady job, more than enough money, and a great insurance plan."

Brandon's last sentence caught Charles by surprise. "What are you saying?"

"I'm thinking about asking her to marry me." Brandon would have laughed at his dad's shocked expression if he hadn't been so serious. "It would give her what she needs to keep Kendra. When the adoption is finalized, we can have the marriage annulled."

Charles held up a hand to stop him. "Married? Annulled?" He took a moment to study his son, as though trying to decide whether he was joking or not. "You don't think that might be going a bit beyond helping?"

Brandon rubbed his temples with his fingertips,

trying to get his mind to slow down so he could think clearly. "There's not a lot of time or a lot of options. I can't think of any other way that gives her as good a chance of keeping Kendra."

Brandon remained silent and Charles watched him for a moment, at a complete loss for words.

"Dad?"

"I'm going to bring something up that I think you are purposefully avoiding in this whole situation."

"And that would be?"

"What if you end up falling for her and she never feels the same way?"

"I would be doing this to help her keep Kendra. Then I would have to let her go." Brandon heard his own words as he spoke them, but he knew it might not be as cut and dried as that. Yes, he wanted to help Rachel keep Kendra. He wanted her to know stability, to know that she wasn't going to lose the only family member she had left. He also knew that he had been attracted to her since before this whole thing had started.

The fact that he was her instructor had made it easy to ignore that pull. Without that teacher/student boundary, it was not going to be as easy. The extra time he'd spent with her in the last week only proved that point to him. If anything, he'd been drawn to her even more. What would happen if he were around her every day for weeks or even months? He didn't realize he'd been holding his breath and he let it out slowly. "If that happens — and I'm going to do my best to go at this with my own feelings on the back burner — I can handle it. It won't be easy, but I'll be fine."

Charles eyed his son thoughtfully. "Brandon, I can't tell you whether this is the way to go or not. But do your mom and I a favor. If this is something you are truly considering, make sure you keep praying about it. As long as you keep your heart open to what He has to tell you, He has an amazing way of closing or opening the right doors."

"And while I wait?"

"Check on her. Let her know you're there for her and you're not going to give up trying to help. If things were so difficult for her growing up, she may not have ever had someone she could count on besides her sister." Charles laid a hand on his son's shoulder and drew him into a hug. "God already knows how things are going to play out." He turned and headed back to the main house.

Brandon knew he wasn't going to turn his back on Rachel. He hoped she hadn't left yet. *Let me have a chance to contact her, God.* His next thought was that he hoped his independent ex-student would even welcome his help. God knew that might be one of the biggest challenges he had to overcome.

~

Rachel resisted the urge to throw something at the wall when she saw that Kendra was watching her. She offered the little girl a forced smile and unplugged the stove. Of course it would die on her. She could call the apartment building manager and have them fix it. But then what was the point? They were being evicted in just over a week, anyway.

"Is it broken?"

Rachel nodded.

"So no more macaroni and cheese?"

Rachel couldn't help but chuckle at the girl's

innocence. "I'm sure we can figure out a way to make your macaroni and cheese," she reassured with a wink. There was no way she was going to let on how serious their situation was becoming. She had exhausted all of her job possibilities. Here she was — broke and out of options. The first court date was approaching fast, and she was no closer to a better situation.

Next to the calendar was the card that Brandon had given her with his cell phone number. A pang of regret went through her as she thought about the last time she had seen him. He was just trying to help, and she had been less than appreciative. Good people were hard to find anymore — or at least it seemed that way to her. She hated to think that she had discouraged his attempt to do something kind for someone else.

Rachel had to look at the calendar to see what day of the week it was. Time had seemed to warp after Ryan and Macy were killed, even more so now that she wasn't attending classes. If she didn't have a watch or a calendar in view, she had to struggle to figure out the date. Today was Monday and she couldn't help but think about where Brandon was going to be that morning.

She picked Kendra's shoes up off the floor and held them out to her. "Let's get ready, sweetheart. Auntie has an apology to make."

Chapter Four

Brandon motioned to the whiteboard. "I have time set aside for a study session on Friday for those who are interested. If you're having any trouble understanding the material, I highly recommend you show up at least for a while. Until then, I'll see you guys on Wednesday." As his students filed out, he began putting his notes and book back into his messenger bag. Footsteps brought his attention to the classroom door.

The sight of Rachel standing in the door, young Kendra holding one of her hands, made him stop. "Hey," he said softly. Seeing her sent a flood of relief through him. Putting his bag down, he took a few steps toward them. He was almost afraid he'd scare Rachel away, and very aware of his heart pounding in his chest. "I didn't expect to see you ladies again."

Rachel met his green eyes with her own dark brown and then focused on Kendra, running her fingers through the girl's hair. "I wanted to apologize for how everything ended last week. I was rude and I want you to know that I really appreciated your help.

You went above and beyond — something most people wouldn't have bothered to do." She looked at him again, her expression genuine. "Thank you."

"It was a rough day, and I never had any hard feelings. I was worried about you."

She nodded. After a moment of silence, she motioned to the door. "I guess we should get going."

"Why don't I take you both out to lunch — it's my treat." *Please, please don't let me scare her off.*

He could tell she was thinking about it, but he could see the wall slowly coming back up. She cleared her throat and looked uncomfortable. "I appreciate the offer, but we should go."

Brandon felt a moment of panic. *God, if her coming here was part of Your plan, You're going to have to help me know what to say.* Rachel looked like she couldn't decide whether to turn and leave or not. He took that opportunity to point to one of the chairs nearby. "Sit down for a few minutes. Please." He thought she was going to say no to that, but she finally agreed. Kendra immediately climbed into her lap and Rachel encircled her with her arms. Kendra blinked her green eyes at him and watched as he turned another chair around to face them and had a seat. "How have you been doing?"

Rachel shrugged. "We're making it." It was clear he wasn't going to get any specific details right now, and with Kendra right there, he didn't blame her.

"Are you sticking around?" Brandon knew he was being forward, but at this point in the game, he didn't think beating around the bush was going to accomplish much more.

Rachel raised an eyebrow at his question. "I've had no luck, and I've got less than two weeks to move.

My options are running out."

Brandon's heart squeezed, urgency filling his gut. "Will you do me a favor?" When she looked at him, her expression guarded, he continued. "Come with me to the orchard this evening and have dinner with my family. We're a crazy bunch and you deserve a break. If nothing else, it'll keep you distracted for a little while. Something tells me you could use a little bit of that." She started to object, but Brandon held up a hand to stop her. "My mom is an amazing cook. And I bet Kendra and Benjamin would have a lot of fun playing together."

Rachel shook her head. "I don't think that's a good idea." She looked down and caught Kendra peering up at her with hopeful eyes.

Brandon lightly placed a hand on her shoulder. "Please." He tried to ignore the warmth he felt at the touch. "You can't pass up a good meal and the chance to hear my brother make fun of me."

That last part made Rachel smile.

"It sounds like fun. Thank you."

Brandon gave her a grin in return.

Thank you, Lord.

~

Rachel sat in the passenger seat of her car. The drive to Brandon's family home was a good thirty minutes, and since she was unfamiliar with the route, she'd agreed when he offered to drive. Kendra was in her car seat, kicking her feet and singing a song about sunshine that they'd taught her at daycare. Macy had loved to sing, too. Hearing her niece's sweet voice was like a balm to Rachel's aching heart. She turned to Brandon. "So your whole family lives in the same house?"

"My family owns a large piece of land. There's a main house that my dad had built years ago, and it's where my brother and I grew up. My parents still live there." Brandon looked over his shoulder and switched lanes. "My brother and I were given a section of the land to build our own homes on. Trent is actually a few years younger than me. He and his wife, Melinda, had a house built on his land shortly after they were married so they live there with Benjamin." He smiled at the thought of his nephew.

"And how about you?"

"I had a house built on my section of land about two years ago. I kind of wanted my own space and had the design drawn out long before then. But on evenings when I'm not at the university, I often drive to my parents' house for dinner. My mom can cook a lot better than I can open a can of soup."

Rachel nodded slowly. "It's impressive you are all so close like that." She couldn't imagine having a house of her own at this point in her life. "What do your parents actually do with the property?"

"A lot of it is left as forest land. We have a large orchard with different types of apples." Brandon reached over and turned the nearest air conditioner vent away from him a bit. "Every fall, we pick all the apples and sell them in area farmer's markets. My mom and Melinda also cook a ton of pies, butters, and things like that which they sell as well. It keeps us all pretty busy from midsummer through the end of the year."

"That must have been such a great place to grow up. I can't imagine actually living in the same place all my life." Her voice was wistful, and she couldn't quite keep the sadness out of it. The way the words came out even surprised herself.

"You moved a lot when you were in foster care?"

She nodded. "Yes. I was young when I entered the system, and I was finally able to be adopted by my sister when I was sixteen. In those twelve years, I was shuffled between fifteen different foster homes. No one was mean or anything. I'm incredibly thankful for that. I was just never keeper material."

"I can't even imagine. I'm sorry you've been through so much."

They rode in silence the rest of the way until Brandon turned off the main highway and onto a small road. "This is where our land starts. The main house is just ahead over that hill."

Rachel admired the dense trees that surrounded them. Ferns and other shrubbery grew at the bases of the trees and moss covered much of the bark on the trunks. When they topped the hill, a beautiful, two-story white house stood in front of her, the green trim and shutters accenting the design perfectly. She gasped. "Wow. What a gorgeous house."

Brandon grinned. "It is, isn't it? My dad is an amazing designer."

They parked in front of the garage. Rachel stepped out of the car, breathing in the scent of the earth and the trees around her. She'd always lived in the city. It was amazing the effect the country air was having on her already as she felt some of her stress evaporate.

Kendra scrambled out of the car, her eyes growing wide as she took in the view around her. "There are so many trees. Do people and animals get lost in all of the them?"

Rachel chuckled. "I'm sure they learn their way around. But since we're new, you and I had better stay together." She winked at her young charge, who grinned at her in return. Rachel held the small hand in her own as the girl bounced up and down with excitement.

Brandon opened the front door and called inside, "It's Brandon. I'm home."

There was the tapping of feet and a little boy with straw-colored hair came into the room with a grin. "Unca Brand!"

Brandon laughed, scooping the boy up in an arc and hugging him. "Hey, kiddo. Did you have a good day?" He turned to Rachel. "This is Benjamin. Benny this is Rachel and Kendra." The little boy waved at them shyly and Kendra readily returned his greeting.

"Hi." Rachel smiled, then looked up as a man entered the room. He resembled Brandon, but he was shorter by several inches and his hair a bit darker as well.

"There you are, munchkin." He tickled Benjamin and picked him up. "Hey Brand, good to see you." The brothers hugged, and Brandon turned to Rachel.

"Trent, this is Rachel and Kendra. This is my little brother, Trent."

Trent held his hand out to her, and she shook it. "Nice to meet you," she said sincerely. Trent knelt to shake Kendra's hand, making the girl smile brightly.

"Nice to finally meet you, too. Let me take you back here and introduce you to the rest of the family. Everyone is in the living room."

Rachel was glad she had Kendra to focus on, feeling very out of her element. She followed Trent through another room and into the living area, reaching down to straighten Kendra's shirt unnecessarily. It was one of the few shirts the girl had that wasn't getting too small.

Three people stood from the couch and approached them. Trent did the honors. "This is my wife, Melinda, and my parents, Sarah and Charles."

Rachel was surprised when both of the women gave her a hug. By the time everyone had expressed how nice it was to meet her, she was feeling overwhelmed and almost claustrophobic. "Thank you," she whispered. "It's nice to meet you all, too." She looked down at the little girl who was staring at everyone with wide eyes. "This is Kendra," she introduced with pride, smiling at her with all the love she had in her heart.

Sarah waved at Kendra warmly. "Hi, Kendra. I love your long hair. It's very pretty."

"Thank you," Kendra said quietly. "Mama said it looked like nutmeg."

Rachel blinked back the tears that immediately flooded her eyes.

Sarah curled a bit of the girl's hair around her finger. "Your mama was right. It looks just like nutmeg."

That seemed to please Kendra, and she stood a little straighter. Rachel protectively laid a hand on her niece's neck and rubbed her back with her thumb. She managed to get the tears under control. "Kendra looks like her mother."

Sarah gave her an understanding nod. "Then your sister must have been very beautiful."

"She was," Rachel returned the woman's warm smile.

Sarah turned to motion to the living room. "Make

yourself comfortable. The bathroom is down the hall. Would you like something to drink?"

"I'm good for now, thank you. I think I'll take Kendra to the restroom quick, and then we'll be back." Giving everyone a smile, she led Kendra away, looking forward to giving herself a few minutes to get caught up. Everyone was so friendly and welcoming. They truly seemed to enjoy being around each other. *It must be nice,* she thought wistfully.

~

Brandon watched Rachel leave, then turned back to his family. Trent was grinning at him. "Seriously, Trent, don't start." He gave his brother his sternest look and bent to pick Benjamin up again, tickling him until the little boy was laughing hysterically. "Have you been causing trouble today, little man?"

Benjamin shook his head but kept laughing. Brandon set him back down on the floor only to watch the boy leap into the air and bounce off the couch cushion.

Charles gave Brandon a supporting squeeze to the shoulder and Sarah hugged him. "You're doing a good thing," she whispered into his ear.

They made small talk until their guests came back into the room. Rachel took a seat on the couch and Kendra immediately sat on her lap. "Thanks for having us," Rachel told them sincerely. "You have a beautiful home."

Charles nodded graciously at her compliment. "We're glad you could join us. We'll have to give you a tour after we've had dinner."

"I would like that."

Periodically, Sarah would get up to check on things in the kitchen and then return to participate in the general conversation. Rachel asked once if she could help, but Sarah assured her all was under control. Brandon enjoyed watching both Melinda and Rachel with their little ones, and wondered at how much more active Benjamin was compared to Kendra. He was curious whether this was how Kendra normally acted or if she was being exceptionally shy.

Before long, it was time for dinner. After saying a brief prayer, everyone began to eat, murmurs of appreciation over the food heard around the table. Rachel helped Kendra with her roasted potatoes and chicken.

"Dinner is amazing, thank you." Rachel spoke from the chair next to Brandon. "I honestly can't remember the last time I had a good, home-cooked meal."

"We're so very glad you could join us, Rachel," Sarah said with a genuine smile. "I hope you know that you and Kendra are welcome here any time."

"I appreciate that." Pink crept into her cheeks and she moved her head so that some of her hair hid her face. Her attention returned to her niece.

Brandon had come to realize that was Rachel's way of hiding when she felt uncomfortable. He wanted to put her at ease, but was afraid anything he might say would make it worse.

After cleaning up, Trent, Melinda and Benjamin gave everyone hugs and said their goodbyes. "We've got an early morning tomorrow — we need to get this monster his bath and into bed at a good time," Melinda said, poking her son in the tummy with a smile. "It was so good to meet you, Rachel."

"You guys, too," Rachel responded, waving to Benjamin.

It was noticeably quieter after the trio had left. Brandon couldn't help but wonder how much more lively it would be once their new baby was here. He could imagine Benjamin and a sibling teasing each other and playing together.

"Would you like a tour?" Charles asked. When Rachel agreed, all five of them headed outside, Kendra holding tight to her aunt's hand.

They showed their visitors the gardens behind the main house. There was a vegetable garden that had something growing in it year-round. The flower garden behind the house was especially colorful this time of year. "I suppose I've always had a bit of a green thumb," Sarah admitted, a smile gracing her face.

"This is amazing." Rachel inhaled, clearly impressed.

Brandon watched her stop to admire some roses that were a deep purple in color. Kendra tugged on her hand and her aunt bent over to let her whisper in her ear. "Of course you can smell the rose, my girl." Kendra beamed at her and then leaned forward ever so carefully until her nose, which turned up slightly at the tip, touched the rose petals. She sniffed, and pleasure filled her little face.

"It smells just like purple."

Brandon thought the comment was adorable.

Charles stepped forward, took his pocketknife out, and gently cut the flower off at the stem. After removing all thorns, he handed it to Kendra. "A pretty flower for a pretty little girl."

"Oh, thank you! Thank you!" Kendra cradled the

flower in her hands as though it was the most precious thing she'd ever received.

"Yes, thank you," Rachel repeated softly.

They continued walking, showing Rachel the entrance to the orchard and then circling back to the house. By the time they'd returned, Kendra had gotten tired and Rachel was carrying her.

Sarah pointed to the north. "Trent's house is that way, and Brandon's is the other. You can't see them, but they're not more than ten minutes from here."

"That must be so neat to be this close together." There was no missing the wistful note in Rachel's voice.

Brandon felt his heart break at the loneliness hiding in there, too. He watched as Rachel held Kendra close to her chest, rubbing circles on her small back. The girl yawned widely and then rested her head against her aunt, still holding the rose gently in her tiny hands.

"Looks like she's getting sleepy." Sarah reached over and wrapped a few strands Kendra's hair around her index finger. "We were going to sit and watch a movie if you'd like to join us. It's kid-friendly. Otherwise, we completely understand if you need to get back."

Brandon was shocked when Rachel immediately agreed to the movie. They went back into the house and settled in the living room as Charles got the movie set up. Rachel sat in the rocking chair with Kendra curled up in her lap. Sarah had placed some wet paper towels in a plastic bag and then put the rose's stem inside so the flower wouldn't wilt. Kendra still held tightly to the rose.

The movie had barely begun when Kendra's eyes

fluttered shut, the dark lashes composing peaceful crescents against her sweet face. Rachel placed a kiss on her sleeping niece's cheek.

Realizing he'd been watching them, Brandon averted his gaze to the TV. When the movie was over, he and his parents stood to stretch, and they noticed that Rachel didn't move. He walked to the recliner and smiled softly when he saw that she had also fallen asleep. Sarah came behind him and put an arm around his shoulders. "It's getting late. Why don't you see if she wants to stay the night in one of the guest rooms upstairs?"

Brandon nodded. She pressed her forehead to his and gave him a smile before leaving the room with Charles.

Brandon crouched down in front of the chair, lightly touching Rachel's arm. "Wake up, Rachel."

She stirred and opened her eyes, sitting up quickly. "I'm so sorry," she started, her face coloring. "I guess I was tired."

"No need to apologize. But it's getting late. My parents have a spare room upstairs they said you and Kendra are welcome to use. If you want, you can sleep there, and I'll take you home in the morning."

Rachel was going to object, but when her eyes met his, Brandon saw her reconsider. He studied her face, saw the range of emotions she experienced. Without thinking, he brushed some of her hair behind her ear, not at all surprised that it was as soft as he had imagined.

She gave a small nod in agreement. He led Rachel upstairs and pulled the covers down on the bed so that she could place Kendra in the middle. "If you need anything, please let someone know. Goodnight."

"Goodnight," she echoed, and it was with some effort that he turned and left the room, closing the door behind him.

Downstairs, he found his parents sitting in the den. "Rachel and Kendra are settled in the guest room." He sat down in one of the chairs and sighed, rubbing his hands over his face. "Thanks for having them on such short notice."

"Anytime, Brand, you know that," Sarah said. "Rachel is so sweet — and lost."

Charles nodded. "It doesn't sound like she'd ever been in a healthy family situation, or a stable one, until her sister. She's done very well considering all she's gone through."

"I agree. I don't know if I could have gone through something like that and do as well as she has." Brandon frowned. "Losing Kendra would kill her."

They sat in silence for a time until Brandon spoke again. "If I told you I was going to ask her to marry me tomorrow morning, what is your first reaction? Seriously, the very first thing you think or feel?" He regarded his parents, truly respecting their opinions.

Charles glanced at his wife, then back to his son. "I think you feel more for her than maybe you realize. We don't want you to be hurt." He reached for Sarah's hand. "At the same time, we feel like she was put into your life for a reason. While we're nervous about it, we feel at peace with your decision."

Sarah nodded in agreement, her eyes bright with tears. "God is using you to help this woman and little girl. We have to trust that He knows what He's doing, and whatever happens, it's according to His will."

Brandon could hear his heart thudding in his chest.

"We'll pray tonight. I doubt I'm going to be sleeping much. I have no idea how she's going to react." He thought about how independent and stubborn Rachel was and a small smile tugged at the corner of his mouth. Yeah, he had a pretty good idea how she was going to respond. It was more a matter of whether he could convince her to change her mind.

Charles and Sarah had some ideas they wanted to bring to Brandon's attention that might help Rachel. They prayed together in the den before Brandon left to go home, promising he would be back at eight the next morning for breakfast.

Chapter Five

The first thing Rachel noticed when she opened her eyes was how the sun came through the lace of the curtains. It was as though the light were painting tiny little flowers on the wall opposite the window. It took her a full five seconds before she remembered where she was. She eased up onto her elbow so she could look at her niece. Kendra was still fast asleep, arms bent and hands clasped together by her chin.

With a glance at the clock on the side table, Rachel saw that it was just after seven. She knew Kendra was going to be hungry, and she could feel her own stomach rumble as she changed out of the night things Sarah had brought up for her and back into her clothes from the day before. After brushing her hair out, she braided it starting at the nape of her neck. By the time she finished brushing her teeth, Kendra was stirring. "Hey, sweetie. You ready to get some breakfast?"

They found Sarah in the kitchen. "Good morning!" The older woman greeted Rachel brightly.

"I hope you slept well."

"I did, thank you. Probably better than I have in a long time. I appreciate you and Charles for letting us sleep here last night. I hope we didn't overstay our welcome."

"Not at all. You're welcome any time." Sarah took some toast and placed it on a plate before slathering it with butter. She smiled at Kendra. "Do you like toast with jelly?" Kendra nodded. "Good! I have three kinds of jelly, and you can pick whichever one you like best."

Rachel got Kendra set up at the table and helped her spread some strawberry jelly on her toast. She turned back to Sarah. "Is there anything I can do to help?"

"I think Charles should be down any minute, and Brandon was going to come over for breakfast, too. I've got just about everything done here, but thank you. You sit there and have a piece of toast with your niece."

Rachel smiled and did as she was asked. "It must be so nice to have both of your sons living so close to you."

"It is. I'm very thankful for it. I've always been far from my parents and I prayed that I could be closer to my own children."

"Where do your parents live?"

"They're both with the Lord now, but they did live in Nebraska." Sarah gave Rachel a sympathetic smile. "Losing your parents is never an easy thing."

"No, it isn't. I'm sorry to hear about that."

Sarah poured some orange juice into a glass. She was placing food on the dining room table when both Charles and Brandon walked in. "Good morning, you two," Sarah said, giving them each a kiss. "Sit down, we're about ready to eat."

"Did you sleep well, Rachel?" Charles asked.

"Very well, thank you. And thank you again for your hospitality, I appreciate it."

She looked at Brandon, and he met her gaze with a smile. Rachel couldn't help but feel more comfortable with him than she did most people. That thought alone made her nervous. She didn't like relying on someone else, and if she got too comfortable, it would be easy to do just that. She was going to have to be more careful.

They ate breakfast in easy conversation. As they were cleaning up, Brandon came up to Rachel and touched her arm lightly. "Do you mind if we go for a walk here in a few minutes? I wanted to talk to you."

Something in his eyes made her hesitate, though she couldn't put her finger on why. "We should be getting back soon."

"It won't take long and it's important. Please."

Rachel wanted to take Kendra and head back home, but after all that Brandon and his family had done for her, she felt like she didn't have a choice. She nodded her agreement. "I should go get Kendra's jacket from the car. It's been a little chilly in the mornings."

~

Brandon felt like his heart was in his throat as he led the way outside. He thought they could walk to the pond. The path was pretty this time of year, and it would give him a few minutes to work up the courage he needed to ask her. He didn't think he'd ever been this nervous before. *God, please give me the words to say and the strength to say them. If this is Your will, soften Rachel's heart to the idea.*

"It really is so peaceful here," Rachel commented at his side. She breathed in deeply. "It reminds us just how small we are in this world, doesn't it?"

"It does," Brandon agreed. He took in God's handiwork around him and suddenly felt humbled. *No matter what happens, Father, thank you for what You have done in my life.*

As they approached the pond, he led them to a bench overlooking the still water. "Let's sit here for a minute."

Rachel did as he suggested. Kendra was admiring a small patch of flowers growing a few steps away in the grass. Rachel watched her niece for a moment, then turned to him. "What's going on?"

Brandon willed his stomach to quit doing flips as he began. "I want to help you and Kendra. It isn't fair that this is happening to you guys. You should stay together — you both deserve that."

Uncertainty marched across her face. He said another silent prayer and took a deep breath.

"Marry me, Rachel."

As soon as the words were out, she jumped to her feet. He stood with her, holding a hand out to try and get her to wait. "Please, listen to me. I've got health insurance, the house, the job. It would hopefully be enough for you to get custody of Kendra. My parents were going to hire someone this year to help with the orchard. Melinda doesn't need to be climbing ladders to pick apples in her condition, and she's been tired lately between the pregnancy and Benjamin. They said they would love to hire you, which means you can put some more money away and Kendra can stay with you." He smiled toward Kendra who had a small fistful of flowers and was on the search for more. "When it's all over and the adoption is finalized, we can have the marriage annulled if that's what you want."

"If that's what I want?" Rachel looked at him as though he'd suggested she hold her arms out and fly. "I would think it would be something we'd both want." She put a hand to her head and closed her eyes, massaging her temple. "If I even agree to this crazy idea. This is insane." She pointed a finger at his chest. "You're insane!"

"I just know I've been thinking about your situation, praying about it, and I can't come up with any other way to give you a chance to keep Kendra."

Rachel's expression was quickly changing from surprise to annoyance. "Look, I appreciate your sense of responsibility, even if it is misguided." She fingered her braid and then tossed it behind her. "But I've been on my own and I've survived. I'll be fine here, too."

"And if you have to run?"

"Then I'll start over. I used to do it all the time when I was a kid. I'm no stranger to it." The fire in her eyes dared him to contradict her.

Brandon could tell he was treading on thin ice at this point. He sent up a silent prayer for God to help him choose his words wisely. "I have no doubt that you are capable of starting over. You're one of the strongest people I've ever met." He took a step closer to her. "But think about the details. If you run with Kendra, they're going to put out a warrant for your arrest for kidnapping. When you get to your new destination, how are you going to find a job? You're not going to be able to use your real name if you truly want to hide. They're going to want your Social Security number, to see your driver's license." He paused, knowing that his words were upsetting her. But they had to be said. "You're not being realistic. Going someplace and starting over like that is going to be complicated. You'll have to figure out how to create a whole new identity."

"I can do that. I will find a way." Rachel clenched her fist and opened her hand again. She turned back to the pond, working her jaw as she thought. Brandon paused for a few moments, knowing that she was going to have to think through it all to make a decision herself. He watched as she focused her attention on the little girl nearby.

"Rachel." He waited for her to look at him before continuing. "You deserve better than to have to go through the rest of your life in hiding. You deserve more than living out of your car or watching over your shoulder every time you take Kendra to the park."

~

Brandon's last words hit Rachel hard. He was right about one thing. If she had to take Kendra and run, she would always wonder if someone would recognize her or find Kendra at school and take her from her. She wasn't sure she would ever be able to rest easy.

Did she really have to choose between running for the rest of her life and marrying a man she didn't know? Was that even a choice? She sat back down on the bench, sighing quietly. Kendra ran up to her with a bright smile on her face and presented a ragged bouquet with a flourish. "They are beautiful, my girl! You are so good at finding pretty flowers!"

Kendra's face beamed with pride. "Thank you! I'm going to go find more!"

Rachel continued to watch Kendra for a few minutes. Unable to look at Brandon, she said, "I can't tell you how much I hate this." Brandon rejoined her on the bench but said nothing. "Except for my sister, I haven't relied on anyone. I wasn't the type of kid who got adopted, I wasn't the type of person who others sought out as a friend. So I've learned to blend in, to not draw attention to myself. I've been content to be invisible, and I've learned to get along fine on my own. I don't want to need anyone else."

"Aren't you lonely? Don't you ever get tired of doing everything by yourself?"

She shrugged at Brandon's words. "Does it even matter?"

Brandon made a disgusted sound and stood quickly. Rachel looked up, surprised to see the anger on his face. "Yes, it matters! Do you even hear yourself?" He glanced over at Kendra and lowered his voice. "I know you've been through a lot, and I sympathize. I can't imagine dealing with the things you've had to as a child. Are you fighting for what you want for your life? Or are you taking what is handed to you and admitting defeat? Because it seems to me you're playing the victim and you're trying to hide."

"You don't know me, Professor Barlow. You certainly have no right to tell me that I'm a coward."

Brandon groaned, clearly frustrated. "That's not

what I meant! Look at her — look at Kendra. What do you want for her future? Wouldn't you rather she grows up to be the kind of woman who knows what she wants, who is confident enough in herself to know when to rely on herself and when to let someone else in?" He ran one hand through his hair, glancing up at the sky as though he were trying to find the right words. He took a deep breath and knelt, placing himself at her eye level. "Rachel, you are the strongest and one of the most independent women I have ever met. I have no doubt in my mind that you can do what you set out to do."

Rachel couldn't take the intensity of his gaze and looked away, the range of emotions going through her too difficult to process. A moment later, Brandon gently lifted her chin with his hand to bring her eyes back to his. "Let me ask you a question. What are you scared of?"

His green eyes studied her as tears immediately filled her own. She willed herself not to cry. As she had been doing the last few weeks, she reminded herself that she was too strong for that. She took a deep breath to compose her thoughts. "I'm scared they're going to take Kendra. I'm scared that if they do, for the first time in my life, I will be truly alone." She swallowed. "I'm scared of going into some kind of crazy arrangement with someone I barely know, no offense." *And I'm scared that, once you or any of your family get to know me, you'll all walk out of my life like everyone else has done in the past.* But she didn't dare utter that last thought.

Brandon gave her a small smile. "None taken." He moved back to the bench again, resting his right ankle on the opposite knee.

She looked at him out of the corner of her eye. "I know you have this unstoppable urge to save damsels in distress. But what is this really about?"

He chuckled, but when Brandon looked at her, his eyes were serious. "It's about helping. It's about reaching out to another of God's children when they have a need. You say you're happy being invisible? It's about showing you that you're anything but invisible and that you matter a great deal to God and to a group of people who only want to help you."

Rachel cradled her head in both hands, not sure she could believe what he was telling her. She turned her head just enough to see him. "And what about your family? I'll be taking advantage of them, and of you. The last thing you need is to have to share your house with a couple of strangers."

"You aren't taking advantage of us, not if we're offering help first. If you had walked up to my parents' house, knocked on the door, asked for money and to move in, that would be different. We all genuinely like you both and want to help however we can." Brandon moved to angle himself on the bench so that he could face her better. "Look, you've had to tell me a lot of things you haven't been comfortable talking about. I want to be completely honest before you make your final decision."

Oh, that's a great thing to say to make me more at ease. There was a big part of Rachel that wanted to tell Brandon she was done and didn't need to hear anything else. There was another part of her, however, that was curious about what he might say. And that's why she found herself nodding for him to continue.

"I've been attracted to you since before any of

this started."

Rachel held up a hand to stop him. "What?" She knew her voice sounded incredulous and she didn't even care. "Is that why you're doing this? And since when?"

"No. Rachel, how I feel about you is not a factor in why I've proposed. It's strictly to help you and Kendra." Brandon's eyes begged her to believe him.

"Since when?" she asked again, more insistent.

~

Brandon raised an eyebrow at the woman sitting next to him. Did she want to get into this now? He rubbed the palms of his hands on his pants. "Since you and Jake Starling got into that debate in class."

Rachel looked at him with wide eyes. "For two months?" Her voice was low, so much so that he almost didn't hear her. "I had no idea."

"Rachel, you were my student. You weren't supposed to know." Brandon took a deep breath. "I would be lying if I said I didn't look forward to spending more time with you and getting to know you better."

A breeze came through, and Rachel crossed her arms against the chill that promised true fall weather was on its way. "My first instinct is to tell you 'no' and to disappear." She looked at Brandon and when his expression remained open and genuine, she continued. "But I'm running out of time. And I'm out of options."

Brandon watched Rachel. He could see the war she was waging within herself as her eyes revealed the range of emotions that she was going through. She stood again and walked closer to the pond. Brandon stayed on the bench, resisting the urge to follow her. He continued to observe her, his heart filled with peace as he silently prayed for all of them. When she turned to look at him, he stood.

She shoved her hands into the pockets of her jacket. "Okay."

He stepped forward, his heart pounding. "You're sure?"

She gave him a small laugh. "No. This is insane, and I think you're probably the craziest of us all." Rachel paused. "But I truly appreciate your offer. Kendra and I will do our best not to disrupt or change your life, and we'll leave as soon as the adoption process is complete."

Brandon didn't respond to the comment because right now he refused to think about a time when she would walk out of his life. He gave her a reassuring smile. "You're welcome here as long as you like. When are you supposed to be out of your apartment?"

"Friday."

"Monday we'll go and get the marriage license." He surprised himself by how calmly he was speaking and how matter-of-fact his words sounded. Inside it was a whole different story as he realized that, in many ways, no matter how this played out, his life was going to be changing forever. "I'll get things arranged at the courthouse for Friday afternoon so we can get the legalities of the marriage set. Meanwhile, pack up your apartment, and we'll get you settled in my house on Thursday so you'll have all of your things here."

Rachel was nodding. "I think that'll work well. It

won't take me long to get things packed. We don't have much."

"I'll need you to write down your full name as well as Kendra's, your Social Security numbers and anything else you can think of. Then next week we'll have to work to get all of the records of the marriage so we can have official papers ready for your court date. I'll also get you and Kendra on my insurance. Do you still have my cell phone number?" At her nod he paused, watching her silently for a moment. "Are you okay?"

"I think so." Rachel pierced him with a serious stare. "You can change your mind any time here, you know."

"I'm not going to change my mind."

With that, he motioned to the trail and they started back to the house, walking side by side in silence as Kendra skipped ahead with her flowers. When they reached the house, Brandon opened the front door for Rachel and Kendra. Charles and Sarah were sitting in the living room and stood when they came in.

Brandon felt his parent's eyes on him, questioning him. He gave them a silent nod to let them know Rachel had agreed.

Sarah went forward and gave Rachel a hug. "Sweetie, welcome to the family. You know we're here for you no matter what."

"Thank you," Rachel said sincerely, her eyes tearing up again.

The women went to get some paper so Rachel could write down all of the information she had for Brandon. Meanwhile, Charles gave his son a hug. "We'll keep praying."

Chapter Six

Rachel drove the three of them to get the marriage license on Monday. Brandon spent the following two days trying to get everything squared away. He chose two rooms across from each other for Rachel and Kendra. He taught his class, got things arranged at the courthouse for Friday, and procured help from Trent Thursday to get all of Rachel's things from her apartment.

He was sitting in the passenger seat of Trent's pickup heading for Rachel's apartment. His brother had been more than supportive about everything and remained positive about the situation. "Give her time, Brand. She's going to fall for you."

Brandon tossed him an annoyed look. "I have to move forward like that isn't going to happen, Trent. I barely know the woman. I may find I am less attracted to her when I do."

"Do you really believe that?"

"Absolutely." But the look Brandon shot his brother told him that was anything but the truth.

Trent laughed and gave him a nudge with his

elbow. "Give her time, big brother."

They pulled up in front of the apartment, got out together, and knocked on the door. Rachel opened it for them. "Hi there," Brandon greeted her.

Rachel smiled back. "Hi." She looked at Trent. "How are Melinda and Benjamin?"

"Doing good, thanks. A busy week."

"I know what you mean." She stepped back and waved them in. "I've got everything ready. Thank you guys so much."

Brandon met her eyes as he walked into the house, giving her a smile. He was shocked when he saw the pile of six or seven boxes in the living room. "Is this it?"

"This is it."

"Is there furniture in the bedroom?"

Rachel shook her head. "No, we've been sleeping on an air mattress. I have that rolled up in one of the boxes. And we can leave the couch. It's old and falling apart anyway."

Trent and Brandon exchanged glances. Brandon could tell his brother was just as surprised as he was. It didn't take them ten minutes to carry everything out and put it in the truck, securing it with rope so nothing would shift during the drive. He knew that there hadn't been a lot in the apartment when he was there for the CPS meeting, but he had assumed there were at least beds in the bedrooms.

They agreed that Rachel and Kendra would follow them to the house in her car. "Wow," Trent said when they were in the truck. "She really has gone without for a while."

"Her car isn't in great shape, either. I noticed the other day that it sounded like the engine needed some work. I'm going to make sure to turn that around while she's with me. If she leaves, she'll be doing so with more than she's coming in with." Brandon's words were laced with determination. His heart ached for the woman driving behind them.

"I'll get a few of Benny's things and bring them over. They are just sitting in the closet, anyway."

"I appreciate that. Thanks."

~

Rachel stared, wide-eyed, at the two-story house in front of her. The siding was a deep brown with red brick accents. The large covered porch led up to the front door while green vines climbed the posts. "It's beautiful," she whispered.

Her words made Brandon smile. "Come with me, and I'll show you around."

The first floor consisted of a large living room, kitchen, dining room, bathroom, and a den filled with more books than she had seen anywhere outside of a library or bookstore. Upstairs, there were two bathrooms and four bedrooms. Brandon led her to two at the end of the hall. "This one can be yours, and right across is Kendra's."

Trent had followed them up with a box from the back of the truck. "I'll swing by with a few other things for Kendra's room here in a little while."

Rachel shook her head. "This is too much, guys. Seriously. We can share a room. We've been doing it all this time."

Brandon was insistent. "You'll both sleep better if you have your own rooms."

She had her doubts but didn't argue any further.

Rachel walked into her room and caught her breath. Everything from the curtains to the bedspread was cream with blue accents. The window overlooked a pasture where two ran through the grass. There was a dresser, and the bed looked more comfortable than any she'd slept on in a long time. Kendra tugged at her hand. "It's all your favorite color, Auntie." Rachel's eyes misted. It was like the rooms she imagined having as a child. And it was all hers.

She felt a hand on her arm and pivoted to look at Brandon. His eyebrows were drawn together in concern. "Is something wrong?"

Rachel smiled. "No, it's perfect. Thank you."

Kendra wanted to see her room so they went next door to find a smaller area that was brightly decorated in yellow and white. Kendra smiled brightly. "It's a banana room!"

Brandon chuckled. "Do you like it, kiddo?"

Kendra nodded. "Oh yes. Thank you!"

~

Friday passed Rachel by like a blur. She hardly saw Brandon in the morning as he was on his way to the college to teach his class. He told her that he'd be back mid-afternoon to pick them up and go to the courthouse.

Rachel worried about what to wear. She knew it wasn't a real wedding, yet she hesitated to wear the same shirts and jeans that had become her typical attire.

The sound of the doorbell surprised Rachel. She hurried downstairs to answer it, hoping that it hadn't awakened Kendra from her nap. She smiled as she opened the door for Melinda to enter, a dress in her arms.

"I thought you might want to have something pretty to wear this afternoon," she offered, handing it to Rachel.

She held the dress up, admiring the simplicity and beauty of it. The folds of the lilac-colored fabric were light and airy. The sleeves were short with a tiny bit of lace bordering the edges. It was perfect. "It's like you've read my mind. I love it, thank you." Rachel gave Melinda a hug. "I'm so nervous. During the handful of times I imagined my wedding, I can't say any of the scenarios were quite like this. What am I supposed to do or say up there? I feel like I'm going to be lying when they have us repeat our vows."

Melinda's expression was genuinely sympathetic. "I know. All you can do is go into this with an open mind — and an open heart." She looked at Rachel with love and compassion. "We all know what this marriage is for and what it means. But it doesn't mean that God may not have other plans."

Rachel felt better, but she wasn't about to tell Melinda that she didn't put a whole lot of stock in God and His plans for her life. "I'll be glad when it's all over, though."

"Do you need any help? Trent is staying with Benny so I'm all yours if you need me."

Rachel smiled gratefully and shut the door behind them.

~

"When is the baby due?"

Melinda unconsciously cradled her growing

abdomen with her arms. "Late February." She smiled. "Benny is excited about having a baby brother or sister, but I don't think he gets the true implications of it." She laughed.

"I'm happy for you. Are you waiting to find out the gender?"

"Well, it didn't start out that way. But at the ultrasound, the baby was all curled up and the angle was all wrong, so the technician couldn't see anything. She guessed girl, but said she wouldn't bet on it. So at this point, we're going to wait until the birth to find out."

"That's exciting! You look great and you carry the baby very well." Rachel meant it. Melinda was tall and thin. All of her baby weight was in the front. She didn't look like she had gained an ounce of weight outside of what the baby had added. Her sister, Macy, had been the opposite. The poor girl had been miserable, gaining weight in her face and hips. At the end of the pregnancy, her ankles and wrists were even swollen. She doubted that would be an issue for Melinda.

"I appreciate that." Melinda seemed to hesitate. "I think it's great how you're taking care of Kendra like you are. She's a lucky little girl, and I know your sister would be so proud of you."

"Thank you," Rachel said, her voice just above a whisper. She wondered what it would be like to experience pregnancy and birth, to hold her own newborn against her skin. As soon as the thought entered her mind, she blocked it out. It wasn't in the cards for her. She had to focus on Kendra.

Rachel looked at herself in the mirror. The lilac dress fit her perfectly, hugging and flowing in all the right places. The hem tickled her ankles and made her feel pretty — feminine even. Something she hadn't felt in a long while. Today may be the last time she dressed up like this, and she was going to enjoy the feel of the light fabric and the V-shaped neckline.

She left her long, black hair to fall in cascades over her shoulders and down her back. Melinda used a straightener to give her hair even more shine than it normally had, and she'd brought her some white sandals to wear with the dress. "What do you think?" Rachel twirled once, nerves taking flight in her stomach.

"You look lovely," Melinda said with a grin. "I didn't realize your hair was so long. It's gorgeous like this. You should leave it down more often." They heard Kendra's voice floating down the hallway. "I have some flowers if Kendra would like to carry them for the service. She can be your flower girl."

Rachel liked the idea. "That would be perfect. Thank you."

She looked at the clock and knew that everyone was going to be there shortly. Rachel helped Kendra change into the one dress that she owned — a pretty white and pink fabric with plenty of lace at the bottom of the skirt. She weaved in a single French braid down the left side of her head and fastened it with a piece of ribbon. "You look so pretty, Kendra!

Kendra looked down at her dress with a pleased expression on her face. "Thank you, Auntie! Your dress is so pretty, too. I wish I could wear it when I get big."

"Thank you, honey. Are you ready to go?"

At her niece's nod, they walked out hand in hand. When she entered the living room, she was surprised to see everyone looking up at her. As she heard murmurs of approval and claps from Benjamin, she felt her face turn a deep red. When her eyes locked with Brandon's, it was clear she had nothing to worry about. She caught a glimpse of the appreciation in his eyes before he schooled his features and approached her. To say he looked handsome in his black slacks and cream-colored, button-up shirt would have been a terrible understatement. His startling green eyes seemed to capture hers.

"We had better get going." He offered one arm to her and a hand to Kendra, who took it shyly. "Shall we?" Brandon leaned in close enough so that only Rachel could hear what he was saying. "You look stunning."

~

Brandon was awestruck when Rachel had appeared at the top of the stairs. Breathless, his heart pounding, he couldn't believe he was going to be marrying this woman that stood before him. Watching her come down the stairs was like watching an angel whose hair shimmered like silk.

Now, with her small hand laying in the crook of his arm, he stood before the judge at the courthouse. They repeated their vows in turn, his family watching. Kendra stood next to Rachel, a variety of flowers in purples and whites clutched in her delicate little hands.

He felt the weight of the ring as he placed it on Rachel's finger. He knew that it was primarily to help build the illusion of the marriage for CPS, but couldn't deny the significance in the motion. Giving her that ring meant offering Rachel his protection and a place in his home. God willing, it would lead to a situation where Rachel could raise Kendra without fear of losing her only family.

That's all this was supposed to be. Then why did he feel like he was handing his heart over to her as well?

"By the power invested in me, I now pronounce you husband and wife. You may kiss the bride."

Rachel inhaled sharply, her hand gripping his. Brandon bent and softly touched her lips in a kiss that he knew was supposed to only be for show. In fact, his mom made sure to photograph the moment to be printed and displayed in Brandon's home for CPS visits.

But it was a kiss he was never going to forget, and it sure felt like a lot more than a pose for a picture. He pulled her into a brief hug. Did the kiss effect Rachel in the same way? Brandon drew her hand onto his arm and turned them around to present his new bride to the family.

~

They all headed to a local steakhouse to eat dinner after the short courthouse ceremony. Sarah had declared the day deserved a celebratory meal, and Trent had teased her, saying she just wanted a night off from cooking. The meal was accompanied by conversation, mostly surrounding the coming fall weather.

"What goes on with gathering apples? What all do you make from them?" Rachel used her spoon to swirl the mashed potatoes around on her plate. Most of them had already gone to Kendra and so she set them aside in case the girl wanted more.

Charles swallowed his bite of steak before replying. "Gathering apples is a long-term process. We started gathering some of those that were ripe early in July. McIntosh is the majority of the ripe apples now, but we're starting to see a few Red Delicious."

"And then we girls will start to can and bake until we won't want to see another apple for a year," Melinda continued. Sarah joined her in laughter but nodded her head in agreement.

Rachel glanced at Brandon who was sitting next to her and then over at Sarah. "I'm not a bad cook, but I'm afraid I've never done any canning. I'm a quick learner, though."

"You'll be fine," Sarah assured her. "Believe me, there will be more peeling, coring, and cooking than canning going on. We make pies, apple butter, and a number of other items that we sell at the Farmer's Market. Charles and I will take care of that part, and we usually go over there every Saturday morning and sometimes Sunday evenings too. Most of it sells well, and of course we keep some for our families."

Rachel smiled. "I think it's neat that you do all of this. To work together as a family and spend so much time outside — that must be nice."

"It is," Charles agreed. His gaze wandered as he took in his family. "I am a blessed man."

Rachel found her mind running, hoping there would be plenty for her to do to earn the money they had promised to pay her during the next couple of months. If there was one thing she was sure of, it was that she was going to make them believe they had gotten their money's worth. She felt like she was taking enough in the way of handouts from this family, and she wouldn't acquire any more than was necessary. A hand on her shoulder brought her eyes up to Brandon's, which brimmed with concern. "Are you okay?"

How long had she been sitting silently in thought? Apparently longer than she realized. She gave him a reassuring nod. "Yes, I'm sorry. Just thinking."

He smiled in understanding and moved his hand from her shoulder to pick up his drink.

They all finished dinner as they talked about the work they would be doing over the next few weeks.

~

Back at the house, Brandon helped Rachel get Kendra inside. It was getting late and Kendra had fallen asleep in the car so he knew Rachel would take her right up and get her ready for bed. She was cradling the sleepy girl in her arms as he closed the front door behind them. When he turned, she was looking at him. "Thank you. I appreciate everything you've done for us. I know you're sacrificing a lot right now."

Brandon watched her disappear around the corner and could hear her walking quietly up the stairs. He took the leftovers to the fridge then headed for the den, turning the television on. By eleven he'd heard no sound from upstairs so he turned everything off and headed for bed.

Sleep was a long time in coming. Brandon thought about the week ahead and how it was going to be the same as always — and yet very different.

Saturday morning, Brandon awoke after falling asleep in early dawn. He dressed and headed downstairs. It was nearly eight thirty, and he imagined

Kendra had been up a while wanting to eat breakfast. He found both ladies in the den. Rachel had the morning paper and was looking through it while Kendra was laying on her tummy on the floor, Candy sitting with her, as she looked at a book.

Brandon sat down next to her. "Did you and Candy sleep well, Kendra?"

She nodded. "Yes."

"Good, I'm glad to hear it." Brandon glanced at Rachel. "How about you? Did you need anything else for your room?"

Rachel smiled kindly. "I have everything I could possibly need. And I slept fine."

"Did you get something to eat?"

Rachel shook her head. "I'm not hungry. I fed Kendra, though."

"You should eat something. Even if it's just a piece of fruit."

"I'll be fine."

Brandon didn't push the issue, but he was concerned because it seemed like every meal he had been around her for, he had to insist that she eat. She wasn't a skinny woman, but he thought she could afford to gain a few pounds.

"What are your plans for today?" Rachel asked him, setting the paper down.

"I need to help my dad with some fencing, which is going to take a good part of this morning and afternoon." Brandon moved from the floor to a chair nearby. "I'm sorry to have to disappear so early after you move in. I wish I could stay." She shrugged but didn't say anything. Brandon changed the subject for her. "What are you going to do?"

"I don't know. We'll probably stay here. I don't

want to be in the way."

Brandon thought about how hard this must be —
to suddenly live in a home that he had only seen for
the first time the other day. He knew he would feel
like a guest and how uncomfortable that would be. If
he were living around people he knew so little about,
he doubted he'd handle it with as much grace as
Rachel was.

"You don't have to worry about being in the way.
If you don't want to stay here alone, I'm sure you
would be welcome over at my mom's house. Or
Trent's. If you would rather stay and make yourself
familiar with everything here, that's fine, too." He
studied her, but couldn't guess which choice she was
leaning towards. "You can come with me if you'd like,
but it'll be a long day of fence work and not very
interesting." The truth was, while Brandon would
have liked to have any excuse to spend the day with
her, he would have been more worried about Kendra
getting too cold. The area of fencing had little tree
coverage, and it was supposed to rain this afternoon.
He wished he didn't have to go and mess with the
fence at all, but it was something they couldn't put off
any longer.

"We're okay here, I think." Rachel looked in the
direction of the kitchen. "I'll try to make sure
everything goes back where I found it."

Brandon laughed, and when she gave him a
puzzled look, he explained, "Cooking for myself is
pretty much making a sandwich or heating a can of
soup. You change anything you want to in the
kitchen."

"And what about house cleaning?"

At that question, the back of Brandon's neck grew

warm. "I admit that I hire someone to come and clean once a week. I'm not here enough to warrant more than that."

With that admission, Rachel's face brightened. "Great! I can at least save you some money there. Cancel your cleaning lady, and I'll take over all that while I'm here. Between that and cooking, at least maybe I can earn some of our keep."

Brandon had a lot of mixed feelings about that. He didn't like that she felt she had to work around his house to make up for her living there. If it would make Rachel feel more comfortable, however, he wasn't going to deny her that.

"Only do those things if you truly want to. It's not part of your stay here, it's not part of your job that my parents are hiring you to do, either."

Rachel nodded, but he could see she was making mental lists and he sighed.

Chapter Seven

"You have to give her some time, Brand. I can't blame her for wanting to stay busy." Trent held another crossbeam of the fence while Brandon hammered in the nails, hitting them much harder than necessary. "And if you keep going like that, we're going to have to repair our repairs."

"I'm sorry, man." Brandon sighed and leaned against the fence in frustration.

Trent joined his brother. "You know she's been through a lot. She's been fending for herself for a long time. It's better to allow her a chance to feel independent here, to contribute to your family."

Brandon picked up another set of nails and went to secure the other side of the crossbeam. "You're the married guy with a happy wife. I may be coming to you for a lot of help in the future."

Trent smiled at his older brother, amused at their swap in roles. "What would you do if you had met her in a completely different situation and had been drawn to her? Just because you're technically married doesn't mean you're not still at that point in your relationship. Be yourself. Once she's comfortable and feeling more at home, turn on the Barlow charms." He grinned when his brother's ears turned red at the suggestion. "Seriously, Brand. If this was some girl you had met at a store or that a friend had just introduced you to, you would take the time to get to know her. Find out more about her life. Do things together to build up a friendship. The fact that you both signed a marriage certificate doesn't automatically give her a reason to fall in love with you."

Brandon ran a hand through his hair and regarded his brother with a grin. "When did you become so smart?"

Trent shrugged. "Oh, you know, it's a gift." He dodged as Brandon lobbed several pinecones at him.

~

Rachel had just gotten Kendra down for a nap when the phone rang. Feeling a bit as though she were intruding, Rachel picked up the receiver with a timid, "Hello?"

"Hi Rachel, this is Sarah. I hope your day is going well."

"Hi Sarah. Yes, it's going fine."

"Good to hear it! Well, we thought we would have everyone over for dinner tonight if that sounds good to you. Try and give you a few days before you have to figure out where everything is in the kitchen there." Sarah laughed, and Rachel thought dinner somewhere else would be nice. "I think Brandon will be working with Charles and Trent most of the day so they'll likely pop in here at dinnertime. I thought we would eat at six. Does that sound good?"

"That'll be fine, thank you."

They talked about a few small things and then hung up.

Rachel spent the majority of the day finding cleaning supplies, getting familiar with the house, and working on sprucing up the kitchen and bathrooms. By the end of the afternoon, she felt satisfied with her progress.

~

Brandon and Trent finished with most of the fencing and did a quick drive through the orchards. Starving, they headed back to the main house. Charles had mentioned something about steak and potatoes, which was enough to bring any hungry man to the dinner table.

Rachel was visiting with Melinda at the table when Brandon came downstairs. Young Benjamin and Kendra sat next to each other, admiring his rock collection.

After the prayer for the meal, everyone began to eat. Sarah had always said that a quiet dinner table meant happy tummies. Tonight that must have been true, because chitchat was at a minimum and the steaks and potatoes were disappearing fast. Even Rachel was eating the majority of her food. Maybe the country air would be good for her appetite.

When the meal was over and dessert was served, conversation turned to the fencing. "We got most of it done, Dad. Just some more to work on near the eastern side." Brandon took a bite of his apple pie. "I think there's a couple of posts there that are going to need to be replaced."

"I appreciate the help, boys," Charles told them.

"I'll take care of the rest early Monday morning. I bet it won't take too much longer."

"Speaking of Monday," Rachel began quietly, "What time should I show up for work? Should I come here? Or meet you near the orchard?"

Sarah smiled at her. "Come by here at 9 if you would like. We're going to be picking apples most of this week and then starting next week, we'll be working in the kitchen as well."

Rachel must have glanced down at Kendra because Melinda rushed to reassure her. "Benny comes with us all the time. He loves climbing the trees, picking apples, and finding critters." Melinda laughed. "I'm sure Kendra will be fine. There's plenty to do and always lots of shade and snacks. We bring a large canopy and some folding chairs to keep them dry if it rains."

Rachel nodded. She was nervous, not knowing what to expect. She was also looking forward to starting work. Just knowing that she would be able to put some money away for her future as well as Kendra's made her heart feel much lighter.

When everyone had said their goodbyes, Brandon followed Rachel and Kendra out the front door, noticing their car wasn't parked in the driveway.

"We walked," Rachel told him, anticipating his question. "It's too nice of a day not to take advantage of it."

Brandon looked up at the sky and then over to the west as the clouds were beginning to turn a light shade of pink. "We can take my car back. It won't hurt Kendra to ride without a car seat for that short distance."

Rachel agreed, and they rode back to the house in

comfortable silence.

Brandon helped Rachel get Kendra out. "Come on, let's get this little critter into bed before it gets late. Church is tomorrow."

Rachel stopped. "I ... I would rather not go."

That seemed to surprise Brandon. "Why is that?"

"I'm not ready for that right now."

Puzzled, Brandon only nodded. "That's fine. I can stay with you if you like."

"No, you should go. Please. We'll be fine at the house."

Brandon didn't argue but couldn't help but wonder what exactly it was about church that she was so nervous about.

When Rachel returned from getting Kendra in bed, she sat on the chair opposite Brandon and leaned forward, her elbows on her knees. "I've only been to church a handful of times, and it's been a while," she told him in an attempt to explain her reaction. "Please. I hope that you'll go ahead and go tomorrow with your family. And I hope you aren't offended by my choosing not to join you."

He studied her a moment. "Look, if you're worried about whether or not you would be welcome, I want to assure you that everyone would be happy to have you join us. Our church is very laid back." She started to speak then hesitated. Brandon continued. "Maybe someday it'll be something you feel comfortable talking to me about." He tried a different tactic. "Did you ever attend church while in foster care?"

"I had a couple of foster families that took us with them. It wasn't a bad experience, though I always felt a bit like a curiosity." Rachel leaned back in her recliner. "People at church would either wonder if I was one of those trouble-causing orphans they had heard about, or wanted to overcompensate in the other direction, making sure I had extra food or attention. Either way, I just kind of wanted to be like all the other kids."

Invisible. Brandon could picture Rachel as a child, trying to blend in with the other children so that no one knew that she was a foster child or that she might be different. He thought a lot of that had carried over into adulthood. "Being independent isn't a bad thing, Rachel. Neither is standing out in a crowd. The important thing is to be yourself. If you stay true to yourself, it won't matter what others think about you."

"You want the truth?" Brandon motioned for her to continue. "I started out in the foster care system trying to be what my foster parents wanted me to be, hoping that someone would adopt me. After a while, I realized that wasn't going to happen and then I tried not to draw any attention to myself." Rachel paused and looked at him warily. "I hadn't even told most of this to Macy. I don't know why I keep dumping stuff like this on you."

"Maybe what you need is a friend." Brandon watched her as she seemed to find a sudden interest in the arm of her chair. "There's nothing wrong with being independent, Rachel. But there's also nothing wrong with having someone else that you talk to. It helps to be able to share some of the burdens you're carrying."

Rachel met his eyes, a glint of determination challenging him. "What about you? Do you have burdens you share with your friends?"

"I admit that my brother is probably one of my

closest friends. If I'm going to share something, it's usually with him. But I don't share everything." He paused, uncertain about his next words. "I wouldn't dare tell him that I sometimes feel jealous of his family. Or that I wish it were easier for me to let things go like he does. I have this annoying habit of feeling like I need to know what's going to happen next in my life."

Rachel was watching him, and Brandon wished he could hear her thoughts just then. She absent-mindedly pulled her hair back at the nape of her neck and twisted it into a bun of sorts before letting it cascade back down. "Friends, huh?"

"I would like that."

Rachel glanced at the watch on her wrist and stood. "It's getting late. I should probably call it a night. Something tells me Kendra will be up bright and early tomorrow." But instead of leaving, she opened her mouth to say something before closing it again. With a small smile, she said, "Goodnight, Brandon," and headed upstairs.

At hearing his first name on her lips, Brandon couldn't help but feel at least some progress was being made.

~

Rachel went downstairs Monday morning to find a note taped to the refrigerator.

Rachel,
I have to go into work early. Don't let my mom work you too hard today. Remember, make yourself at home.
Brandon

She tucked the piece of tape behind the note and set it down on the counter with a small smile.

It was still early, so she warmed up a waffle with butter and syrup for Kendra and then took the chicken she had gotten out of the freezer the night before and placed it along with some spices into the slow cooker. She added some potatoes and carrots, setting it on low so that it would be ready for dinner. She glanced at the bowl of apples on the counter and considered getting one for herself but changed her mind.

She thought about walking to the main house, but knew that by the end of the day, she would be tired and glad she had driven. So she loaded everything into her old car and headed that way. It took a few seconds longer for the engine to turn over, something Rachel had noticed a few times in the past. She chose to ignore it for the time being. Having to put money out for a car repair was not something she was willing to think about right now.

Sarah ushered them inside with a smile. Melinda and Benjamin were already there. It took them all about twenty minutes to get everything they needed together and then they drove one of the pickup trucks to the orchard.

As soon as Rachel stepped out of the cab of the truck, the mixture of earth and apples warmed by the sun assaulted her senses. She took a deep breath. Yes, she could get used to working out here.

Benjamin quickly began to show Kendra how he could climb a tree, find apples on the ground, and collect sticks. Melinda joked that he was having fun showing off for a girl, which had Rachel laughing.

With the use of two a-frame ladders and large buckets, the three ladies visited as they picked apples and gently placed them into the buckets. Sarah insisted Melinda stay on the ground at this stage in her pregnancy as opposed to climbing the ladders, and Melinda didn't argue with her. Even though the buckets weren't much more than about twenty-two pounds each, Sarah and Rachel carried them when needed. Otherwise, the buckets stayed on the ground near the trees, and the guys would come through and pick them up in the evening.

Rachel enjoyed being at the top of the ladders the best. There was something about being so close to nature that made her feel free. It was almost like she could stay out of the reach of life's storms if she could remain hidden up there in the trees. She noticed a cardboard box attached to the tree and pointed to it. "What's that used for?"

Sarah followed the direction of her hand and nodded at the box. "Those are traps for codling moths. They're one of the main pests we have to worry about with our apples. We put pheromones in the traps on powerful sticky paper to attract the male moths." Sarah pointed out the red tube holding the pheromones. "When the male moths land, they stick to the trap and are unable to get free. The goal is to attract them before they breed in hopes of preventing larvae that bore into the flesh of the apples." She pointed at another tree nearby and there you could see several of the boxes hanging in it. "Some of the trees have more than others. We check them regularly and if there are quite a few moths that have gotten stuck, we know there may actually be a problem. It's a little late in the season for them — we see them more in the late spring and early summer. But with the warmer-than-normal fall so far, it's better to keep an eye on them."

The relaxed, easy conversations she was having with Sarah and Melinda made the work go quickly. She enjoyed hearing about the time that Brandon and Trent had built a tree house and then the ladder had fallen, trapping the young brothers in the tree. At some point, Trent was convinced that a bear was going to get them until Charles had come to the rescue. Rachel laughed openly at the memory the ladies described for her.

"Do you have any siblings, Melinda?"

"I do — two sisters. But they're a lot older than I am. I see them every few years, but we aren't really in touch." She shrugged. "I used to feel bad about that and wished I had siblings around. But honestly, it worked for my family and we're all fine with it." She patted her round belly. "Besides, I have family here now, too."

Rachel let her mind take her back to when she and Macy were kids. Truth be told, she had very few memories of that time. It was almost like all of the memories since entering the foster care system had crowded the others out.

She did remember sitting on one of their mattresses before bedtime and listening as Macy read a story to her. She remembered another time when Macy was trying to brush all of the tangles out of her long hair. But as far as carefree childhood days, she was hard pressed to come up with any.

Rachel had stopped picking apples and had been staring at the tree when Sarah reached a hand out and touched her shoulder. "You seem deep in thought."

Rachel forced a smile. "Sorry about that."

They drove back to the house for lunch and bathroom breaks before heading back out to the orchard again. The kids were starting to get a little worn out and were content to sit in the shade with crayons and coloring books. At 2:30, Sarah stopped them. "I think we should call it a day, ladies. We all have dinner to prepare and you two have kids to take home and get cleaned up." She drew Benjamin to her in a big hug. "We got a lot of apples picked — made a lot of progress. We'll be back out here again tomorrow."

Rachel headed back to Brandon's house feeling completely exhausted. She managed to get in a shower and play with Kendra a bit before she heard a door shut in the driveway. They were playing on the floor in the den when Brandon walked in.

~

Brandon set his stuff down on the coffee table. "How did the day go for you ladies?"

Kendra rewarded him with a smile. "We picked a million gillion apples, and Benny showed me how to have sword fights. He's a nice boy. He saved me from a hopper that was trying to eat my leaves."

Brandon raised an eyebrow at her big explanation of all they had done that day. He looked at Rachel to find her smiling at him in amusement. When Kendra quit talking, she filled in. "I think she had a lot of fun out there. The day went by fast, and I think every muscle in my body is going to rebel against me in the morning." With that she stretched her arms and winced.

Brandon laughed and had no doubt she was right. In fact, he could have told her from experience that she would feel her worst on Wednesday, but figured she would find that out on her own. The third day of doing something new was often the hardest.

The truth was, his Monday hadn't gone fast at all. In fact, it had dragged as he went through his normal routine with one major difference: he had a wife and little girl waiting for him at home. And all he could think about through the day was getting back to the house again to see them.

Kendra pulled out her leaf collection and showed all of the different shapes to Brandon, her story surrounding each one accompanied by animated hand waving and facial expressions.

Brandon caught Rachel watching him and gave her a friendly wink.

Rachel stood quickly to hide the red that was creeping into her cheeks. "I should go finish dinner. I hope chicken with potatoes and carrots sounds good."

"It smells amazing, Rachel. Thank you."

Not long later, they were sitting at the kitchen table. Brandon pointed his fork at his plate. "This tastes great, and it's so nice to have more than a can of soup when I get home. I do appreciate all that you've done."

Rachel shrugged. "I tossed it in the slow cooker. I didn't do much." But his compliment did coax a smile from her.

"I've seen enough to show me you do know how to cook. Who taught you?"

"It was one of my foster mothers. I think I was around ten or so. She was a chef — or at least had been. She was in her sixties when I knew her." Rachel set her fork down on her plate and looked out the window as she recalled the memories. "She was really sweet — one of my favorites. She told me that learning to cook was important and that I would be glad to have the skill."

Brandon could tell there was more to the story. "What happened?"

"She ended up falling and injuring her hip. Not long after that, I was sent to a new foster home. I know it wasn't in her control, but not being adopted by her was kind of the turning point for me."

"You had a hard time opening up to foster parents after that," he guessed.

Rachel nodded slowly. "I did." She blinked quickly and turned her attention back to him. "What about you? Sarah is an amazing cook, yet it doesn't look like you've inherited much of that." Her eyes twinkled with the tease and Brandon raised an eyebrow in amusement.

"No, I sure didn't. Let's just say that when it came to cooking, I wasn't a very good student." He gave her a wink and scooped up another forkful of potatoes.

Chapter Eight

Brandon waited in the den while Rachel put Kendra to bed upstairs. He was glad when he heard her footsteps as she came back down to join him. "How was your day?" she asked.

"It was fine. Nothing exciting, but everything went smoothly. Class still doesn't quite seem the same without you, though." He paused. "So tell me something. You were just starting your first year of health science. Were you thinking about going into nursing?"

Rachel shrugged. "I wasn't sure if I was going to go into medical coding, sonography, or continue into nursing."

"What would influence the decision?"

"Time and money," she said frankly. "I couldn't afford to end up with that much in school loans. I was hoping to get a couple of years of college under my belt." She laughed dryly. "Apparently that was hoping for too much."

Brandon watched as she fiddled with the hem of her shirt. "Were you going into the medical profession because it was something you really wanted to do?"

Rachel looked at him, uncertain. "Honestly, no. I chose it because I knew I could get a job in that field when I was done."

Brandon had suspected as much. She'd been focused, and had gotten good grades. But she didn't seem to have that passion for the subject that he saw from most pre-med students. "And if you could do or be anything, what would you choose?"

Rachel's expression became guarded. "I'm not even sure."

"I think you know," he prodded her gently.

"Maybe." She paused. "I think it's a discussion left for another day, though."

Brandon knew he wasn't going to get any further with that line of questioning and turned to the topic of apples. It wasn't even ten when Rachel began to look so tired that she excused herself to go up and get some sleep.

~

Tuesday had brought with it a lot of rain. Unlike the more common mist or light drizzle, this was a heavy rain, and it had fallen like that most of the day. By the time Brandon was ready to head home, the streets were waterlogged. He was thankful he'd left early.

He was about three miles from home when he spotted a car on the side of the road up ahead. It only took a moment to recognize it as Rachel's. As dread twisted his stomach into knots, he stopped his Camry behind her vehicle. After looking into the windows, he saw that the car had been abandoned, and that made Brandon even more nervous.

He got back into his car and slowly continued down the road. It was about a mile later that he saw a figure walking along the shoulder up ahead. When she heard the car's engine, she stopped and turned. Brandon's relief at seeing Rachel with Kendra in her arms was huge. He stopped the car again and got out, hurrying around the front. "Are you two okay?"

Rachel nodded at him. "I needed to run to the store for something to go with dinner and on the way back, the car stalled. I couldn't get the engine to turn over again."

Brandon noted that Kendra was wrapped up in Rachel's raincoat, and that Rachel had only her jeans and long-sleeved shirt to protect her from the rain — both of which had been soaked through some time ago. He reached for Kendra and cuddled her to his chest. "Come on, let's get you home."

He led Rachel to the car and opened the passenger door so that she could climb in. "I'm going to get your car all wet," she protested.

"Rachel, it's not a big deal. Get in before you freeze." Brandon waited for her to get seated and then handed Kendra to her before running around to the driver's side. Once they got back to the house, he helped them in. Pointing to Rachel's room, he told her, "You go in and get changed while I take Kendra in here and get her into some warm pajamas and a blanket." He knew Rachel must have been miserable because she only nodded in agreement and disappeared.

Brandon was relieved to see that Kendra had stayed quite dry in the raincoat. He got her pajamas off the bed and changed her into them, throwing a blanket around her shoulders for good measure. "How would you like some hot chocolate to warm up the inside, too?"

Kendra's eyes grew wide as she nodded. "I've never eaten hot chocolate before!"

He carried the girl downstairs and got her set up at the kitchen table. He'd just finished heating the water when Rachel came into the kitchen. She'd changed into some dry clothes, her wet hair hanging down her back. She was rubbing her hands together in an attempt to warm them up.

"Auntie! Brandon has hot chocolate. Have you ever ate hot chocolate before?" Kendra's excitement brought a smile to Rachel's face.

"I have, but it's been a long time! It sure sounds good on a chilly day like today, doesn't it?"

Kendra nodded emphatically.

Brandon fixed three mugs, adding some milk to Kendra's in order to cool it down a bit so the girl could start drinking it right away.

Rachel cupped the mug in her hands, drawing warmth from it. "Thank you. Both for the hot chocolate and for finding us."

"I'm glad I left work early today. I hate the idea of you both walking all the way home in this." He took a sip of his hot chocolate. "We'll get your car towed in tomorrow and find out what's going on with it." Brandon observed Rachel. She was still sitting with her arms close to her body and her shoulders slightly hunched. "Are you feeling any warmer at all?"

"Some," she told him.

Brandon left the room and brought back one of his thick jackets. "Here, put this on and see if it gets rid of the chill." He helped her shrug it onto her shoulders and then scooped her hair up with his hands to pull it to the outside.

"Thank you." Rachel tucked her hands into the pockets, her gaze locking with Brandon's for a moment until she returned to her hot chocolate. Brandon followed suit, but the vulnerability he had seen in her dark eyes stayed with him.

~

"Scrapbooking always seemed overwhelming to me, but you make it sound like a lot of fun. I wish they offered less variety in the craft stores. How someone's supposed to narrow down the choices is beyond me." Rachel glanced over at Kendra. "I suppose I should learn or get a camera or something so I can record Kendra's life."

Melinda nodded. "It was crazy overwhelming at first. Trent teased me for a long time about the boxes of papers and stickers. Now that I kind of know what I'm doing, I can narrow down what materials I need before I step foot in the store. If you ever want to get started, I can give you a hand."

"I appreciate that. Thank you."

Sarah traded places with Rachel and climbed to the top of the ladder so she could reach some of the higher apples. "I did photo albums for a long time, but I'm probably behind by 10 years now. I have photos organized in boxes." She blew some of her graying hair out of her face. "Finding the time to actually put them in books has been the real issue."

Rachel replaced the full bucket with an empty one. Kendra and Benjamin had taken to rock collecting that afternoon and were quickly filling up the pails that they were given. Kendra complained twice about her head hurting, and Rachel noticed that she wasn't quite up to her usual energy level.

"What are your hobbies, Rachel?" Melinda was asking.

Rachel thought about that question and grew quiet. A bunch of different things ran through her head and she came to a realization. She had no hobby. No major interests. Her face must have drawn a blank because both of the other women had stopped to look at her. She felt her cheeks flush. "I guess I don't have one. How sad is that?"

"It's not sad, Rachel," Sarah responded. "You've had a lot going on, and I'm sure you've put everything else before your own interests. Hopefully you'll be able to focus on some of the things you enjoy once you've gotten custody of Kendra."

Rachel nodded, but she wasn't so sure she believed that. What person didn't have a hobby or interest? The thought bothered her the rest of the day as they picked apples and then as she and Kendra walked back to Brandon's house.

By the time they got there, Kendra was in total meltdown. Every little thing was setting her off, from dropping Candy on the driveway to Rachel having to set her down in order to open the front door. Upon entering the house, Brandon peeked in from around the corner. "Wow, rough day?" He reached down to pick up Kendra, but she shook her head, her cheeks wet with tears, as she reached up for Rachel. So instead, he took Rachel's bags from her so that she could pick the girl up.

Rachel was rubbing her back and holding her

close. "You're home early," she commented, thinking that at this point he probably wished he weren't. "Let me try and calm her down, and then I'll get dinner started." She kissed Kendra's head softly. "I'm starting to think she's not feeling well. She wasn't herself all day."

Brandon waved her off. "I'm home early to get your car towed to a mechanic in town. I've got this. You tell me how you like your eggs, and I'll make us some breakfast for dinner."

Rachel agreed. She rocked Kendra in the living room and it didn't take long for the girl to fall asleep in her arms.

~

Brandon wasn't completely sure what awakened him. He looked at the clock, trying to focus on the 3:17 that was staring back at him. Rubbing his hand over his face, he was about to drift off to sleep again when he heard Kendra begin to cry. He knew immediately that was what he'd heard in the first place. He expected her to quiet down, but instead the crying intensified. Sitting up in bed, he reached for the shirt that he had tossed onto the night table and pulled it on over his head.

As soon as he opened his door, he could see the lights were on at the far end of the hall. As he approached, he spotted Rachel in Kendra's room, attempting to rub the little girl's back. The sound of Kendra crying tugged at his heart.

The moment Rachel realized he was there, she frowned. "I'm so sorry we woke you. I've been trying to get her quieted down but she won't relax at all."

Rachel placed a kiss to the girl's forehead. "She says her head hurts and she's really warm."

Brandon walked forward, stopping next to Rachel. He reached a hand out to touch Kendra's face and immediately agreed. "I have a thermometer in my bathroom. Let me go grab it."

When he returned, he checked her temperature using the thermometer on her forehead several times before announcing, "Looks like about 102. Do you have any fever reducers that you can give her?"

"I've given her acetaminophen, and it hasn't seemed to make any difference." Rachel sighed in frustration. "And apparently I can't do anything to make her feel better."

"Do you have any ibuprofen? I remember Trent once saying that you can alternate the two to get a fever down." When Rachel shook her head, he tried to think. "Why don't we try a cool bath, see if maybe that might help her feel better?

Ready to try just about anything, Rachel nodded.

Kendra cried, shaking her head in protest, as Rachel stripped her down and Brandon filled the tub with tepid water. As soon as Rachel lowered her into the water, Kendra cried even harder. "It's c-c-c-cold, Auntie. It's too c-c-c-cold."

"I know, honey. But it'll help you feel better. Soak for a few minutes, and then we'll get you out."

Arms crossed in front of her, Kendra finally agreed to sit down in the water and leaned against one edge of the tub while Rachel poured water over her shoulders and brushed her hair back off her forehead.

Brandon caught Rachel's brown eyes with his own. He gave her a nod of encouragement, and she returned her attention to Kendra.

They let Kendra sit in the water for a few more minutes and then wrapped her up in a towel. Rachel got her dressed while Brandon went down and filled a sippy cup with cool water. When he got back upstairs, Rachel was rocking her niece in a chair in Kendra's room. The girl was looking sleepy, but fought the drowsiness with everything in her. He handed the cup to Rachel.

Taking a seat on the bed, Brandon watched as Rachel rocked Kendra, her eyes shut as she listened to the girl's breathing. It wasn't long before the little one was asleep, and Brandon thought Rachel might have drifted off as well because the rocking chair had stopped moving. Quietly, he stood and lifted Kendra from her arms. The girl sighed as he gently placed her on her bed. Rachel hadn't even shifted, and he knew she had to be exhausted. He noted that it was nearly five in the morning.

"Rachel," he whispered, touching her shoulder. When Rachel didn't stir, he pulled the covers back on the bed in her room. He eased Rachel into his arms, a little alarmed by how light she was. Once he had her situated, he made sure to pull the blankets up over her sleeping form. Brandon paused, admiring Rachel's peaceful face. Her eyelashes were long and dark, a contrast to her light skin. Her nearly black hair fanned out over the pillow and the comforter rose and fell softly as she breathed. "Get some sleep, sweetheart." Brandon left the room to get a last hour or two of sleep himself before he needed to be up for the day.

~

Rachel's head was pounding even before she

opened her eyes. With a groan, she rubbed her face with one hand. A quick look at her watch told her it was after nine in the morning. With a start, she jumped up and quickly checked on Kendra in her room, relieved to see the girl still sleeping peacefully. With a feeling of panic, she realized she was already late for work.

A piece of paper caught her eye, and she lifted it off the side table.

Rachel,

I talked to my mom and Melinda, and they know that Kendra's been sick. Please take the day off to take care of Kendra and don't worry about the job. There'll be lots to do later. Melinda said to let her know if you need something to help Kendra if that fever doesn't stay down. You have my cell number. Please don't hesitate to call me if you need anything at all. I'll try to get home early tonight, and I'll bring dinner with me.

Brandon

Rachel felt a combination of relief that she could stay there and take care of Kendra, but also guilt that she wasn't holding up her end of the bargain with the job. She felt Kendra's face, content that she didn't feel feverish. Taking advantage of the fact that Kendra looked like she was going to sleep a while longer, Rachel grabbed a shower.

~

Brandon held the pizza box with one hand while he unlocked the front door. When he entered the house, all was quiet. He left the pizza on the kitchen table, set his stuff down, and headed upstairs. As he started down the hall, he could hear Rachel's voice float to him. He got closer to Kendra's room and he could make out the words of "Hush Little Baby." He stopped outside the door and listened, the sweetness of Rachel's voice washing over him. It wasn't just that she was singing to Kendra, or that she was singing on key, that struck him. Her voice was truly beautiful.

Not wanting to disturb her, but also unable to resist, he took a few more steps forward and leaned against the doorframe. Rachel was rocking her niece as she sang. When she reached the end of the song, she placed a sleeping Kendra on the bed, lovingly tracing her nose with a finger. "I love you, Kendra." The whispers were barely audible.

Rachel turned to leave the room, spotting Brandon in the doorway. Pink colored her cheeks as she stepped past him and then waited for him to follow before heading downstairs.

"Is she still feeling better tonight?"

Rachel nodded. Brandon had called once during the day and Sarah another time to check on the two of them. "She never had a fever higher than 99 all day, thank goodness. I kept her on fever reducers though, just to be sure. I guess it must be a cold."

"Very possible. There's a lot of stuff going around combined with your getting stuck in the rain and having to walk."

Rachel followed him into the kitchen and spotted the pizza box. "Oh, you were reading my mind."

Brandon grinned as she got a couple of plates out and didn't hesitate to open the box, diving right into the pepperoni pizza. "Has that little girl been keeping you on your toes today?"

Rachel nodded. "This is the first time she's slept all day. She refused to take a nap but wanted me to either hold her or sit by her the rest of the day. We watched a lot of TV this afternoon." She took a big bite of pizza, a moan of appreciation escaping her lips. "The good news is that hopefully she'll sleep solidly tonight, and we can get back to normal tomorrow."

"If you need another day off, it won't be a problem."

At that, Rachel held her hand up. "No, I'm not going to take another day off. I can't. Your parents hired me, and I'm not going to let them down."

Brandon wanted to object, but he held his tongue.

"CPS called," Rachel began, her whole demeanor changing. "The first court hearing will be a week from Friday."

He mentally calculated the days. That only gave them one weekend before the meeting. "The new insurance cards should be in the mail, but I'll call and make sure they're on their way. I'll pick up a copy of the marriage license this week. If it's not ready, it should be early next week."

Rachel nodded but didn't say anything.

"What are you thinking about?" he asked.

"What if this doesn't work?"

Brandon put a hand gently on top of one of hers. "It will work. You need to have faith. You have to go into this court hearing positive that you're in the right and that everything is going to be fine."

Rachel gave him a doubtful look. "How do you do that?"

"What?"

"Have faith? I'm messing your whole life up, yet

it's all sunshine and roses. All life has taught me is that, no matter how much you want something or wish for something to be, it very rarely works out that way. Sooner or later, your boat is going to sink in the storm, and you have to start all over again." She removed her hand from beneath his. Her French braid had started to work itself loose, and there were strands of hair hanging by her ear. Rachel unconsciously wrapped them around her second finger. "I realize I sound jaded, but at this point, the only thing I have faith in is that life will find a way to screw me over."

Brandon dusted crumbs off his hands but remained silent.

Rachel gave him a pointed look. "You're not going to tell me about how, if I had more faith and wasn't so negative, things would be fine?"

"Something tells me you would rather I didn't." He gave her a wink and let the subject drop.

Chapter Nine

Brandon didn't get a chance to spend much time with Rachel through the following week. He usually saw her in the evenings for a short time, but that was about it. He knew the ladies had been picking apples like mad and that Rachel and Melinda had taken Benjamin and Kendra to the pond on Thursday afternoon. It sounded like Rachel was starting to adjust, and he was glad to hear it. He found himself wishing he didn't have to spend a majority of Saturday morning and early afternoon helping Trent and his dad with more repairs.

The mechanic contacted him and was able to fix the carburetor in Rachel's car. It hadn't been as expensive as he feared it would be, and he paid the bill. He and Rachel went to pick the car up Thursday evening so she would have it available again. She'd visibly paled when he told her how much the repair bill was and insisted on paying him back with her first paycheck.

Friday evening came, and it was already nearly six when he got home. Exhausted, he got a helping of the chicken fajitas Rachel had left in the slow cooker and then headed to the den to start grading papers for his class. He was so glad to be done — it'd been a grueling week. It was 7:30 when he looked up at the clock and started to worry about where Rachel and Kendra were. Wishing — not for the first time — that Rachel had a cell phone, he picked up his own and dialed his parent's house.

When Charles answered, Brandon quickly filled them in on the situation and asked if they knew where Rachel and Kendra happened to be. Sarah got on the phone then. "Brandon, she left here around 3 and said she was going to go walk through the orchard before she went home. You might want to head over there and look. Do you want us to go, too?"

"Let me go check, Mom. I'll let you know if I find her or need any help."

They agreed to the arrangement and Brandon pulled his shoes on before running out to his car and heading towards the orchard. It wasn't dark yet, but the sun was getting quite low in the sky and he couldn't ignore the worry that was building in his chest.

However, once he reached the orchard, it didn't take long before he spotted Rachel on a ladder under one of the trees. She turned when she heard the engine, and her tired expression made him sigh. He saw Kendra sleeping on a blanket nearby so he resisted the urge to talk until he got closer. "What on earth are you guys still doing out here?"

Rachel shrugged and reached for another apple. "I'm trying to make up for missing work on Tuesday when Kendra wasn't feeling well." She looked at him as though that should explain everything, but he felt impatience at her words. It must have shone in his eyes because she gave him a confused frown.

How did he make her understand that she didn't have to earn her keep because she took all of one sick day? Brandon put pressure on his temples as he tried to funnel his thoughts into something he could express. There were a lot of reasons he could give her for not being out here at this time of the evening, but he could see she was already on the defensive. He released the breath he'd been holding. "It's going to be getting dark soon. Why don't we get this baby girl home and in bed?"

He thought she was going to argue with him, but she finally nodded and started her climb back down the ladder. He helped her with the apples in her arms and together they got everything loaded and headed back to the house.

~

Rachel remained silent as they pulled into the driveway. She whisked Kendra upstairs and got her into bed. Her own stomach was complaining loudly about her lack of food. In fact, she hadn't eaten anything since lunch, and she knew that had been a mistake. Her head was throbbing, and she was feeling a bit dizzy. With a sigh, she headed back downstairs, the smell of the chicken fajitas drawing her to the kitchen.

Brandon was already there, putting a large portion on a plate for her and getting some cheese out of the fridge to go with it. He handed it to her. "You skipped, dinner didn't you?"

"I didn't skip dinner — I'm eating it late." Rachel

placed the meal on the table and pointed to it. She turned quickly to get something to drink and immediately regretted the action. The dizzy sensation she'd felt upstairs overwhelmed her, and her knees buckled.

In one movement, Brandon caught her around the shoulders. He scooped her into his arms and carried her to a chair near the table.

All Rachel could do was fold her arms on the table and rest her head. Eyes closed, she willed the world to stop spinning. Brandon knelt beside her so he could see her face. "Do I need to get you to a doctor?"

"No." She held up a hand to stop him and lifted her head off her arms. The dizziness was still there, but it had lessened quite a bit. "I just need a few moments." She paused, her face flushing. "And some food."

Brandon moved into the chair next to her, and she could feel him watching her intently as she used a fork to get several bites of the fajita mix. Her hands were shaking as she put some of the meat onto a tortilla and rolled it up. She'd skipped meals in the past, but never reacted like this before. Now she was feeling incredibly embarrassed.

At least he had the good sense to not lecture her until she'd gotten some food in her system. She had just finished the fajita and washed it down with some cold water when he asked, "Did you eat lunch?"

Rachel nodded. "I had a half sandwich," she admitted.

At her response, Brandon immediately stood and started to pace to the sink and back. "That's all?"

Rachel shrugged. "I was trying to get as many apples picked as possible."

"That's not a good enough reason."

"I missed a day of work. I needed to make up for that since your parents are paying me."

Brandon shook his head. "No, it doesn't work like that. And you know it doesn't. It won't hurt you to stop for 30 minutes to eat something. With the kind of physical work you are doing right now, you can't get away without eating like you could before. Would you deny feeding Kendra so you could pick a few more apples?"

Rachel's anger immediately boiled to the surface. "Of course not! What kind of person do you think I am?" Her face heated and she dropped her fork on the table.

"Not allowing yourself time to eat is just as bad, Rachel. What if you'd gotten dizzy while on that ladder out there and fallen, breaking a bone? What if you two had been stuck out there all night, and you had to lay there while Kendra was scared, unable to get her home?"

Rachel stared at him, unable to think clearly. "I.... I hadn't thought about it like that."

~

Brandon silently prayed that his words would have an impact on Rachel. He truly couldn't understand why she denied herself food when there was plenty of it. "I'm going to check in with you each day about what you've eaten until this habit of skipping meals is gone." She started to protest, but he shook his head. "It's that or I'll mention it to my mom so she can make sure you're eating lunch when you guys take a break during the day." The look of horror in her eyes told him he had said the right thing.

Reluctantly, she nodded. "I won't skip any more meals."

Brandon's relief was immeasurable. "I'm going to hold you to that." He stood to leave and paused. "And after having to hunt for you twice now, I'm seriously buying you a cell phone." He bent to press a light kiss to the top of her head before turning and going into the den to finish up a few things before bed.

It'd been a week since they got married and one thing was certain — he still had a lot to learn about his new wife.

~

Saturday dawned bright and clear. When Brandon came down the stairs, he heard Rachel's voice and Kendra's laugh. Both did a world of good and made him smile. "Hey, you two. Sounds like you're having fun."

Rachel looked up at him with a grin. "We are! Kendra woke up in a very giggly mood." She tickled the girl's toes, and she started laughing again, Rachel close behind her. "We already ate breakfast, but there are some muffins in the kitchen."

"I need to head out to help Dad and Trent. I'll grab one on the way. Thank you."

"We'll be spending lunch and the afternoon at your parents' house so we'll see you over there when you join us all for dinner."

Brandon was a bit surprised but nodded. "Sounds good." He waved, grabbing a blueberry muffin from the counter on his way out.

~

"Brand, grab that two-by-four and bring it over here, please." Charles surveyed the fence line. "I didn't realize how much damage there was on this side."

They worked silently for a time until Trent threw a question in his brother's direction. "So how is Rachel doing?"

"I think she's okay. We've had several good conversations which has been a step in the right direction."

Trent gave his brother a clap on the shoulder. "For what it's worth, I've noticed she's really relaxed and opened up this week. Melinda said they've had a great time working together."

"I'm glad to hear that." Even though they had had a few issues with eating meals and the awkward church conversation, Brandon felt that he'd gotten to know more about her. He hoped she felt the same way about him.

When they finished the repairs, they headed back to the main house. The guys got cleaned up and changed shirts before joining the rest of the family members in the living room. Benjamin spotted them first, hopping up and running to Trent. "Daddy!"

"Hey, buddy!" Trent scooped the boy up and gave him a big hug, lifting him to sit on his shoulders. "Have you been taking good care of your mama today?"

"Yes," the boy said with an emphatic nod.

Brandon chuckled and looked over at Rachel. She was sitting on the floor talking to Melinda, her hair falling loosely over her shoulder. She to pushed it back and hooked it behind her ear. When she turned to meet his gaze, he thought his heart would beat out of his chest. He couldn't get over how beautiful those dark, chocolate eyes were. He gave her a wink and a smile, effectively causing a tinge of pink to touch her cheeks followed by a quick dip of her head to break eye contact. He liked that the smallest gestures brought about that reaction from her.

He went to go sit with her and Kendra, who had been playing on the other side of the room and was running over to join them. "Hi, Brandon! Are you all done with work?"

Brandon chuckled. "Yes, I'm all done with work. How about you? Did you work hard out in the orchard?" Kendra nodded emphatically. "Good! You didn't eat more apples than you picked, did you?"

That got a giggle from Kendra. "Nooooo!"

"We've got a couple of hours before dinner." Sarah stood and started to cross the room. "How about a game of Taboo?"

"That sounds fun," Charles agreed. "I vote we draw names for two teams tonight."

Sarah retrieved the game from the closet and returned as everyone drew straws. As it turned out, it was Melinda, Charles, and Brandon on one team while Sarah, Trent, and Rachel comprised the other. They had to explain the rules to Rachel as she'd never played before. But once she thought she had the rules down, they began.

It wasn't long before everyone was laughing as one person tried to give hints to a word on a card without using any of the obvious words listed. The score was close when it was time for Trent to draw a card. As soon as he saw it, he grinned and turned to Rachel as

Charles began the timer. "Okay, Rachel. Melinda told me about this one. It was what Benny did when you were out at the lake."

Rachel looked surprised. "Ran into? Bumped? Oh! Sideswiped?"

"Yes, sideswiped. Bumped — he did a bit more than that." He laughed, then turned to explain to the others. "Apparently my young son was riding his tricycle when they went to the lake and rode by Rachel, nearly knocking her into the water. I dread teaching that boy to drive."

"Oh, I don't know." Sarah laughed. "Sounds like father like son to me!"

Brandon watched as Trent went through several more cards before their time ran out. He caught himself staring at Rachel more than once, fascinated by how much she'd changed in the last week. She was happy. Content. Most of all, she was having fun.

When the game was over, it was determined that Trent's team won. The food that'd been cooking in the kitchen beckoned to them and Sarah suggested they eat.

Brandon reached his hand down, offering it to Rachel so he could help her up. But once she was standing, he didn't release it. He waited for her to look up and meet his eyes, then he smiled at her. "I missed you today." He gave her hand a squeeze and reluctantly let go.

~

It was Sunday morning and when Brandon came down dressed for church, Rachel's belly did a flip-flop. She caught herself thinking about how handsome he looked in the tan slacks and pale blue pullover shirt. She almost felt bad that she wasn't going to go to church again this week. There were a lot of reasons for that. She didn't feel like she had appropriate clothing. She also wasn't so sure she was ready to be in public, meeting the Barlow's friends, and having to be introduced as Brandon's wife. The thought alone made her feel nervous and she knew her decision to stay at the house was the right one.

When Brandon saw her dressed in jeans and a blouse, she thought she could detect a bit of disappointment on his face.

But if that was the case, he covered it quickly. "I may go riding for a bit this afternoon. I haven't taken my horse out much, and he hasn't been happy that I'm ignoring him."

Rachel nodded. "Of course." She paused, working up the nerve for her next question. "I've never gone riding before. I was wondering if maybe you could show me how some day."

Brandon swung to face her, clearly surprised. Then a pleased look crossed his face. "Of course. Maybe we can go riding one afternoon this week."

She smiled at him. Riding a horse was something she'd always wanted to do. But she also hoped he'd see that he could carry on with his normal activities even while she and Kendra were there.

~

The week went by quickly and Friday afternoon was here before Rachel knew it. Dressing in her best — which wasn't much different than what she wore every day — Rachel expertly French braided her hair and then did the same for Kendra's. Her stomach was in knots as she tried not to let her mind wander with the possible outcomes of the court appointment at three. Brandon said he would be home anytime now so that they could go together.

Brandon's family joined them, but waited outside as they were told only those closely related to the case were allowed into the courtroom for that first meeting.

Rachel was glad to have the weight of Kendra in her arms. It helped her to stay focused. As they entered the courtroom, Brandon reached for her free hand and gave it a supportive squeeze. She didn't object when he held onto it as they found their seats. She spotted Ryan's aunt and uncle as they walked in, looking about as nervous as she felt. They looked at her in turn and found their seats nearby.

Everyone stood as the judge entered the room and the proceedings began. The judge was an older man who seemed kind enough. He gave each of them a smile before beginning, asking them to state their intent with regard to Kendra and why they wished to have custody of her.

Ryan's aunt and uncle, Steven and Jennifer Lawrence, were tearful as they explained that Kendra was the only connection they had left to their nephew and that they felt like they were in the best position to raise the girl.

When it came time for Brandon and Rachel to speak, Rachel willed herself to stay calm and not let tears come into play. "My sister and Ryan were the only family I had, your honor. I've been there every day since Kendra was born. I know that my sister and Ryan would have chosen me to raise Kendra if they'd had the chance. This little girl is the only family I have left. I grew up moving from foster home to foster home. If there's one thing I know, it's the importance of a safe place to grow up and we will provide that for her." Rachel stroked Kendra's hand while Brandon moved closer to put his arm around them both.

The judge thought for a few moments while he looked again at the papers that he held before him. "From this initial gathering, I can see that both parties care about the child and intend to raise her as their own. I need to have some meetings conducted while each of you think about and decide for sure that this is the path you wish to take. We will reconvene four weeks from today. Until then, Kendra will remain in the custody of Brandon and Rachel Barlow."

Rachel felt numb. The good news was that she had Kendra with her for another four weeks. The bad news was that the Lawrences were going to pursue the custody battle, and that made her heart hurt. She squeezed Kendra's shoulder as everyone around her talked. She heard little to none of what was being said. Someone asked her a question, and when she didn't respond, Brandon took her hand in his. "Are you okay?"

"I don't know," she said honestly. "I just want to go home."

Rachel gave Sarah and Melinda a hug, telling everyone how much she appreciated their coming to the courthouse. "Your support means a lot. Thank you all so much."

"Of course, Rachel. We're here for you." Sarah gave her a second quick hug before everyone went their separate ways.

~

The ride home was a silent one and by the time they got there, Brandon was starting to worry about Rachel. Dinner was solemn and little more than chitchat was exchanged. It was time for Kendra to go to bed, so Rachel took her upstairs and he wandered to the den.

When she joined him, he waited for her to take a seat, studying her closely. "Are you going to be okay?" She shrugged. "Come on, Rachel. Talk to me. I know you were hoping for something more definite — but look at the positives. At least the judge didn't decide the Lawrences were going to get her. At least Kendra came home with us tonight. At least you have another month to build up a solid case, to show them what kind of family we can provide for Kendra here. That counts for a lot."

Rachel looked at him and nodded slowly. "You're right. I'm sorry." She took a deep breath. "I'm so used to waiting for the other shoe to drop — it's become a habit."

From what he'd learned about her, he knew that to be true. "Habits can change, Rae." She raised an eyebrow at his use of a nickname but didn't say anything. Brandon continued, "I know things have been rough — I can't imagine going through even a small portion of what you've dealt with in your life. But you have to stay positive. It's better to assume the best of people, and to look for the positives in a situation, than to suppose the worst right out of the gate."

"Is that the end of my lecture?"

"It's not a lecture, Rachel. I'm concerned about

the level of stress you keep in your life." Brandon leaned forward, placing his arms on his knees. "You shoulder everything all on your own when you don't have to. It's unnecessary stress, and I don't understand why you do that to yourself."

Rachel looked offended. "I do have to do it all myself. Because when this is all over, I have to be able to support that little one up there all on my own. And I can't do that if I'm waiting on other people to handle things for me."

Brandon held up a hand. "No, you're right. You're a strong person and you've done such a good job keeping everything going. It's good that you're willing to stand up and handle things on your own, no doubt about that. But there is a difference between being weak and leaning against other people who want to help you."

Her eyes flashed. "There's a hole in your logic there."

"Oh? What's that?"

"Leaning against other people can work, but that assumes they'll always be there for you. Other than my sister, I've never found that to be the case. And even with her, the state made sure she wasn't there for me for a long period of my life." Rachel shrugged as though she had no option but to think as she did. "People come and go — usually go. It was that way as a kid. Maybe not for everyone — but it was true for me. I think some people aren't keeper material, and I'm one of those people." Brandon started to object, but Rachel wasn't done so he leaned back in the couch and motioned for her to continue. "You and your family will see that. The more you'll get to know me, the less likely you are going to want me to stay.

Twenty-six years of experience tells me that it's going to happen, and it doesn't matter how badly I want things to be different."

Her statement completely stunned Brandon, and he wasn't even sure what to say. He knew she was wrong, but how do you explain that to someone who is so intent on pushing people away that she has a skewed view of the truth?

His silence seemed to only confirm what Rachel was thinking because she stood quickly. "I do appreciate everything you're doing for us. It's a big sacrifice. But don't worry, I won't overstay my welcome."

Brandon watched her leave, feeling a mixture of frustration and sadness. Seconds later, an idea came to him. He jogged upstairs, hoping to catch Rachel.

She had just come out of the bathroom and was heading to her room. "Rachel, wait a minute, please."

Rachel turned to look at him, her expression guarded. Brandon hated that he had placed that look there, even if what he said had been necessary.

"You told me that you would like to learn how to ride. How about going on a horseback ride with me tomorrow mid-morning? We can be gone an hour or so and I'm sure Mom would be happy to stay here with Kendra." He waited, not sure if she would accept the offer or not. To his relief, she finally nodded.

"That sounds like fun."

Brandon knew he was grinning like a schoolboy. "Great! You won't regret it." Not willing to give Rachel a chance to change her mind, he turned and went back downstairs to make a phone call.

Chapter Ten

By the time Saturday morning had arrived, Rachel was starting to wish she hadn't agreed to go horseback riding with Brandon. Not because she didn't want to — she'd always wanted to ride a horse — but because the idea of them being alone and having to continue their conversation from the night before made her uncomfortable. Too many things he'd said hit home. She wanted to go on the defensive, to say that he was criticizing. But she knew that wasn't true.

So the goal was to go, have a good time with the horses, and try to keep the conversation light.

Rachel led Kendra down to get some breakfast and found Brandon buttering a stack of toast. "Good morning," he greeted her with a smile.

"Good morning." Rachel got Kendra a glass of orange juice. Brandon took one of the pieces of toast and put a generous amount of strawberry jelly on it before handing it to Kendra.

"Mom is going to come by and watch Kendra for

an hour or so while we go horseback riding. You've
never ridden before, so I'm thinking an hour is
probably going to be plenty. Just fair warning, you
may be sore tomorrow. But it gets better each time."
Brandon looked at his watch. "They'll be here around
ten."

Rachel nodded. "Will I be riding my own horse?"

"That's completely up to you. We'll go out and
you can take a look at them and decide from there.
You're more than welcome to."

Rachel nodded again. Before she knew it, Sarah
had arrived. She went over a few details with her and
then kissed Kendra, leaving her in capable hands.

As they walked to the barn, Brandon explained
some about horses and how one should always mount
from the left side. He cautioned her to never walk
behind a horse because the animal needed to be able
to see her and know where she was at all times. "The
more relaxed you are, the more relaxed the horse will
be."

That last statement had her picturing a horse
bucking her right off its back if it felt as nervous as
she did right now.

"This is Brick," Brandon introduced her to the
first animal they came to, rubbing the horse's face
fondly. She thought the name was fitting as the
coloring of the horse was the same color as the red
brick trim on Brandon's house, with a black mane and
tail for contrast. "This guy is about as gentle as you
get and would be good for your first horseback ride.
Mortar is over there," he pointed across the aisle to a
black horse with matching mane and tail, "and I'll be
riding him today. He's a bit taller and a little more
spirited."

Rachel reached out to Brick and rubbed the soft hair on his muzzle. The horse sniffed at her hand, grunting a little, his eyes watching her every move. He seemed sweet enough, and those eyes looked so peaceful. He also seemed incredibly tall and visions of herself falling off the horse or being thrown would not vacate her mind.

"If you're happy with Brick, I can get these two saddled and we'll get started." Brandon noticed her hesitation. "I know you've never ridden a horse. If you would prefer to ride on Mortar with me today, you can. Then you can take Brick out next time. At least you'll know what to expect and how it feels when the horse is walking or trotting beneath you."

She knew Brandon was trying to rescue her. On one hand, she didn't want to admit how intimidating the idea of riding a horse was. On the other, she thought that riding with Brandon was the lesser of the two evils and so she nodded. "I think that might be a good idea. I'm nervous, and I don't want Brick to sense that. Hopefully your confidence will tip the scales and we can fool Mortar."

Brandon chuckled. "It will be fine either way. You keep poor, rejected Brick here company, and I'll go get Mortar ready to go."

Brandon worked to saddle Mortar. Meanwhile, Rachel kept stroking Brick's nose, whispering, "It's nothing against you. You seem like a sweet boy." The more she petted him, the more relaxed she felt.

"Okay, I think we're good to go. Now let me show you how to mount a horse and then you can try it. I'll be up there to help you, too. Remember, always go in front of the horse to the left side."

He effortlessly stepped into the stirrup and settled

himself in the saddle. He reached his left hand down and she reached to grasp it. He talked her through what to do, and in moments she was seated behind him. Rachel hesitated slightly before putting her arms around his chest.

"Are you ready?" She nodded against his shoulder, and he urged Mortar forward. Rachel tightened her arms around him as the horse walked out of the barn and turned toward the orchard. "I'm going to have Mortar go at a trot for a few minutes. Let me know if it's too fast or if you have any questions."

"Sounds good."

They trotted to the orchard, and then he settled the horse into a slow walk as they meandered through the trees. He put a hand over hers where they were clasped. "You doing okay back there?" he asked, lightly rubbing the top of her hand with his thumb.

"Once you get used to it, it's surprisingly comforting." She wasn't about to tell him that she found him touching her hands to be incredibly distracting as well.

"I agree. Sometimes, if I'm worried about something, I can go horseback riding and it makes some of my problems seem a bit smaller than they were before."

They rode in silence for a while until Brandon spoke. "Are you still angry with me about last night?"

Rachel thought about that a moment. "I was upset last night. Some of what you said still bothers me." She took a deep breath before continuing. "You were right about a lot of things, too."

"Like what?"

"I take on way more stress than I should. I have a hard time letting someone else in." She couldn't help but smile. "Except for a certain guy who seems to insist on banging down the door. He's not giving me much of a choice."

That got a laugh out of Brandon. "Is that a bad thing?"

"No, it's not." Rachel meant that, too.

Mortar was happy to take them on a tour through the orchards and then beyond to the property edge. Rachel had been thinking a lot about their conversation the night before and finally got the courage to speak what was on her mind. "Can I ask you a question? I need an honest answer."

Brandon sounded surprised. "Of course."

"What's wrong with me?"

"What do you mean? Nothing's wrong with you."

Almost wishing she hadn't said anything, Rachel took a deep breath and plunged forward. "Growing up, none of my foster families wanted me. Nearly everyone I've ever loved has left me. Now someone wants me to stick around and I can't ... What's wrong with me, Brandon?"

"Whoa," Brandon said as he halted Mortar, stepping down. He lifted Rachel to the ground, putting a hand on each of her shoulders. "I want to tell you something, and I want you to listen very carefully." He waited for her to look at him before proceeding. "There is nothing wrong with you. Sweetheart, you were dealt a bad hand growing up. You've been through more than I care to imagine. It's completely normal for your heart to be guarded. It's part of who you are — and I wouldn't want you to change a thing." Brandon cupped her face gently with his hands. "There is nothing wrong with you, and I don't want you to think for a moment that there is.

Do you understand me?"

Rachel nodded, desperately trying to keep tears from forming. "Thank you," she whispered. She stared into Brandon's eyes for a moment before he dropped his hands and turned back to the horse. They got settled on Mortar again. As soon as Rachel's arms went around Brandon, he rested his hand on top of hers. Rachel took in a breath to ask another question but stopped herself.

Apparently it'd been clear she was going to speak because Brandon said, "You can ask me anything you want, Rae." He squeezed her hand, encouraging her.

His shortened version of her name temporarily sidetracked her. Or maybe she was looking for a distraction, even if she wouldn't admit it to herself. "You know, after twenty-six years, you're the first person to have ever given me a nickname."

"Any objections?"

She shook her head. "No, I like it." She paused.

"What were you going to ask me?"

Rachel could feel her heart pounding as she tried to work up the courage. "When we first talked about this arrangement, you said something. About how you felt." She paused. "About me." Brandon's thumb stopped rubbing her hand as he waited for her question. "It hasn't been long, but now that you know me more, has that changed for you?"

Brandon removed his hand from hers and gripped the reins with both of them. "Yes. It has changed since I've had a chance to get to know you more."

Rachel's heart sank as she realized that what she'd known would happen had come to pass. As he'd spent more time with her, he'd found she wasn't worth it.

He cleared his throat, drawing her attention back to him. "The more time I spend with you, the more I realize it can't be enough." His words made her physically jolt. "I could probably spend every hour of every day with you and still want more."

Rachel was floored. Did he really say he wasn't tired of her, or that her personality hadn't repelled him? That knowledge was something she had a hard time wrapping her brain around. What was she supposed to do with that information?

~

Brandon waited for Rachel to respond but she was silent. *How much am I supposed to say, God? What is the balance between letting her know that I care and saying too much?* Tentatively, he touched her hand again. "Did I scare you off? Upset you?" He could feel his heart pounding, and wished he could see her face right now.

Rachel took a deep breath. "I don't understand."

Was she asking him to spell it out for her? Maybe she needed to know that someone could care about her — that she mattered. "I'm falling in love with you, Rae." He couldn't do this and not see her. Not know how she was reacting. He halted Mortar and partly turned in the saddle, resting his left hand against the back of the saddle behind Rachel. Her eyes were focused on her hands, which she held clasped tightly in her lap. Hesitating only a moment, he touched her chin and lifted her eyes to his. "I look forward to spending time with you. When I'm at work, I can't wait to come home to you. I enjoy hanging out with you and talking with you." Brandon studied her eyes and then let his gaze travel to her lips. What he wouldn't give to be able to kiss her right then.

Rachel's face flushed pink. "I can't do this, Brandon." She looked like she wanted to run.

"Because you don't think there's any way you could ever feel the same way? Or because you're afraid that you might?" Rachel shrugged but wouldn't answer him. "You asked me how I felt, Rachel. I'm only answering your question." He looked at her, imploring her to answer his question as well.

"Everyone eventually leaves. I guess I always figured I would avoid the heartache."

"Oh, Rachel. By doing all that you can to avoid potential pain, you're missing out on so much more. Like a chance for friendship and maybe even love." He brushed some hair out of her face. He sent up a silent prayer that God would protect their hearts. "Can you look me in the eyes and tell me that you don't think you could ever feel the same way? If you can do that, I'll step back. I'll keep my distance."

Rachel closed her eyes tight and when she opened them again, he could see tears filling them. "No, I can't tell you that." A tear escaped and traced a path toward her jaw.

Brandon didn't think he could speak. The air he'd been holding was released in a whoosh, and he wiped away her tear with his thumb. "Okay." He let his forehead rest against hers for a moment. "Okay."

He turned back in the saddle, waited for Rachel to wrap her arms around him again and covered her hands with one of his. *I know this is going to be a long road, Father, but I praise you for hope. Please open Rachel's heart and guide me so that I don't cause her anymore pain than she's already experienced in her life.*

~

All the way back to the barn, Rachel tried to parse out what she was feeling. Brandon was falling in love with her. She knew that what she'd told him was the truth. She didn't know what she was going to do with the realization, though.

At the barn, Brandon dismounted and then helped her down. "I need to get this big guy cleaned up and something to drink. It'll only take a few minutes."

She nodded. "I'll wait outside." She rested her arms on the top rung of the fence and watched the wind play in the branches of the trees. A few of the leaves were turning yellow, and she knew the rest would follow before too much longer. Rachel heard Brandon leaving the barn and coming toward her. He stopped behind her and rested a hand near hers on the fence. "Are you ready to go home?"

"I think so." She pushed away from the fence and fell in step with Brandon as he led her through the gate and back toward their house. "Can I tell you something?"

"Of course."

Rachel glanced at him and saw that she had his full attention. "The idea of needing someone else scares me."

Brandon reached over for her hand, holding it gently in his own. "It's not so scary if you realize the other person needs you just as much."

Chapter Eleven

Brandon was looking through the newspaper in the den when Rachel joined him after getting Kendra to sleep. She sat on the couch with him, her hands clasped in front of her. He suspected she wanted to say something but was hesitant. Instead of rushing her, he let her have the time she needed.

Finally, she spoke. "I got my first paycheck from your parents today. I thought maybe Kendra and I would go into town tomorrow while you're at church. She's outgrowing everything she owns, and I could use a couple of things, too." She looked down at her jeans that were developing holes in the knees.

He'd thought they needed more clothes but had been reluctant to say anything. He nodded readily. "I think that's an excellent idea. But if you'll wait until after church, I would love to go with you. I can watch Kendra while you try on clothes and it'll be easier that way." The truth was, he wanted to go with them and spend the afternoon together.

To his surprise, she gave him a smile. "Sure, we'll go after you get back from church."

~

They drove together in Rachel's car to the mall where Brandon thought they might be able to get the most variety for both of the ladies in the car. He couldn't help but feel complete as he glanced at the woman sitting next to him and then looked in the rearview mirror at the little girl in the back. *Thank you, God, for Your blessings.*

The mall wasn't too busy yet. Rachel set Kendra down and held her hand. Brandon made a mental note to buy her a stroller, thinking the girl would probably get tired of walking before too long. He might even look for one at the mall if they had any.

"Did you need to shop for anything?" Rachel asked him.

He thought and then shook his head. "Nothing specific, but there are a couple of stores I'll duck into when we see them."

The first stop was a department store. Brandon watched as Rachel looked through the clothing that was the right size for her niece. Kendra was constantly pointing to a shirt to show her aunt. Rachel's decisions seemed to come down to what it said on the price tag. Once she narrowed down the articles of clothing, she would show Kendra the items and let her choose what she liked best. Thirty minutes later, she had found two pairs of pants, two shirts, and some new undies. There was a dress she considered, but as soon as she saw the price tag, she put it back on the rack. Brandon made a mental note of the dress and Kendra's size.

Rachel glanced over at Brandon. "If you want to, you can go look at something you would be more interested in while I do this," she told him. He volunteered to take Kendra over to the tool section so Rachel could look in peace.

Before he did that, he located a small umbrella stroller and purchased it. Kendra was thrilled to climb into the stroller herself and looked at him with a brilliant smile. Brandon's heart melted.

A half hour later Brandon saw Rachel walking toward them. "Hey, you. Did you have any luck?"

"I found a few things," she replied, holding up a bag of items that she'd already purchased. She motioned to the stroller. "She seems to like it."

Brandon smiled. "Yes, and it's easier on our arms and her legs, too. Consider it a gift from me to her, okay?"

"Thank you."

"Come on. Let's go get some lunch."

Brandon was pushing the stroller toward the food court. A group of people came up and they had to stop to let them pass. Rachel reached over to help maneuver the stroller, her hand touching his. Once they got the stroller where they wanted it, Rachel didn't immediately move her hand, which amazed Brandon. Glancing at her, he turned his hand over so that they were palm to palm and laced their fingers together. Yes, a man could get used to this.

They ate some lunch, wandered the mall a while longer, and then decided to head back home. Brandon was visiting with Rachel, their conversation light, when the truck came out of nowhere.

With a screech of brakes and the sound of glass shattering all around him, he only just saw the truck strike the right side of the car. The next realization was the strong dust and smoke from the airbags assaulting his senses, making it feel like the linings of his sinuses were being burned away.

Brandon coughed and then heard Kendra start to cry. His first thought was that at least she was alive and awake enough to cry. He looked to his right at Rachel. She'd started to cough, too, but immediately after that she groaned. "My arm." She moved it, and blood flowed freely onto her shirt. "Kendra!" She tried to twist in her seat to look at the girl but was unable to. "Is she okay?"

Brandon took his seatbelt off and knelt on the console in the middle so he could look at her. Kendra was crying, her eyes wide, but she looked unharmed. He stroked her cheek. "Honey, are you okay?"

Kendra hiccupped. "I'm scared," she said in a whimper.

Rachel spoke from beside him. "Sweetie, I know you're scared. But you need to tell us. Do you have any ouchies?"

Kendra shook her head and hiccupped again. Brandon patted her arm. "Hang in there. You're okay. I'm going to get us all out of here." He turned to Rachel. "She's okay, Rachel. Kendra's fine." He moved to sit back down again and pulled his shirt off over his head. "But you are a different story." Making himself focus, he rolled his shirt up and then twisted it around her arm. There was so much blood, it was difficult to tell exactly where it was coming from. He noticed that Rachel also had a large bump forming on the right side of her forehead.

He was startled when his door opened from the outside. "Are you guys all right in there?"

Brandon coughed. "My wife was injured. I think we're going to need an ambulance. Is the other driver okay?"

The man nodded. "Yes, some bumps and cuts, but he should be fine. I think someone has already called 9-1-1." He heard Kendra crying. "Are you sure the little one is fine?"

"Get her out, Brandon, and make sure. Please."

Brandon got out of the car. He opened the back door and was so glad that Kendra's car seat was in the middle of the back. If she had been on the right side... he didn't even want to think what might have happened. He released the five-point harness and took her in his arms, rubbing her back. "Shhhhh, sweet girl. You're okay." Kendra cuddled into his chest immediately and put her arms around his neck. "You're sure nothing hurts?" Kendra nodded, and he hugged her close. "Good job. Now we need to get your auntie taken care of. She has some ouchies and they're going to take us by ambulance to the doctor to fix them. Can you be brave and help me check on her?" Kendra nodded again. "Good girl."

Carrying Kendra with him, he went back to the passenger side and opened the door, kneeling beside Rachel. "Are you hurt anywhere besides your arm and head?" He checked her face and her other arm.

"My head's hurt?" Rachel reached up to touch the bump and winced, apparently surprised to feel pain. She nodded toward his bare chest. "Are you cold?"

Brandon chuckled. "Sweetheart." He smoothed the hair off her forehead and kissed it. "The ambulance should be here soon." He put more pressure on the shirt to try and control the bleeding. "Hang in there."

Brandon made a call to his dad to let him know what happened and that they would be heading to the hospital. Shortly after that, the ambulance arrived. He held Kendra on his lap as they rode to the hospital. In the ambulance, the EMT worked to find where all the blood was coming from and then covered the nearly four-inch-long gash on her arm with gauze before wrapping it a.

~

Rachel felt as though something were covering her eyes. When she tried to open them, it was like her eyelids were weighed down by something heavy. Everything felt strange and unfamiliar. The sound and the feel of the bed she was laying on all added to her disorientation. She was so cold. With a groan, she forced every ounce of energy she could find into opening her eyes. As soon as she did, a hand covered one of her own.

"Take it easy, Rachel. Don't rush it."

Brandon. Where was she? Memories of the trip to the mall started coming back and then the details of the accident hit her with a force that mirrored the accident itself. She tried to sit up, but the pounding of her head allowed only a partial attempt before she let herself fall back against the bed. "So this is what it feels like to literally be hit by a truck." She closed her eyes again because she had no choice. "I'm so glad you guys are okay. Is Kendra with your parents?"

"Yes, they're out in the waiting room. They were going to take her back to the house, but she became hysterical."

"She left the hospital without her mommy and daddy, and they never came back," Rachel said, her voice catching. "As soon as I can sit up without feeling like I'm going to get sick, bring her in so she can see I'm okay."

"I will, I promise."

"How long was I out?"

"About an hour. You scared me, Rachel. The doctor who took you down for an x-ray of your arm checked on you. He should be back any time here to let us know more."

Rachel felt Brandon brush some of her hair off her face and then hold her hand in his. She was content to rest her eyes. They didn't have to wait long for the doctor to arrive. "You're a lucky young lady," he greeted her. "Can you open your eyes for me?" Rachel did with a great deal of effort and had to endure the bright light he shined at her. "You've got a concussion. It's not bad, but we're going to want to keep you for a few hours to make sure it doesn't get any worse. I don't think any scans are necessary." He paused to jot some information on the clipboard he was holding. She saw him turn to Brandon. "The x-ray came back and everything is fine. No broken bones. We should be able to send her home this evening. But you need to check on her every three hours through the night. Be sure that you can wake her and get her to respond to a question, then she can go back to sleep. If at any point she is unable to answer a question or wake easily, bring her back immediately."

Brandon squeezed her hand. "I'll watch her like a hawk."

The doctor carefully unwrapped her arm. The wound started to seep blood as soon as the pressure had been released. The doctor took a pile of gauze and quickly covered her arm again. "You are very lucky it didn't get a major artery there. You'll need some stitches." He wrote a few more things down. "Someone will be here shortly to sew you up, and then we'll let you rest for a while."

Brandon's phone beeped and he looked at it. "Is it alright if we bring our niece in? She's had some trauma in the recent past related to a car accident and needs to see that Rachel is okay."

"That's fine. I recommend taking her back out before the nurse comes in to stitch that up."

They agreed, and the doctor turned to leave.

~

Brandon saw that Rachel had dozed off again when he returned with Kendra. He sat Kendra carefully on the bed to Rachel's left so as not to bother her injured arm. Kendra immediately laid down next to her aunt. Rachel reached for her and brought her closer. "Come here, baby." Rachel started singing Kendra's favorite song.

Kendra looked at her. "You have ouchies, Auntie?"

"I do, but the doctor will fix them."

"They'll get better," the girl said with emphasis. "Don't worry, they'll get better."

Rachel smiled at her and nodded. "Yes, they'll get better." She kissed her niece's cheek. "I have to stay here for a little while longer. Can you go back to the house with Sarah and play with Benjamin? And I'll hopefully be home tonight. I *will* come home."

Brandon watched the whole exchange, even more sure than ever that the two deserved to be together. He reached for Kendra to take her back out to his parents. Once he got that settled, he hurried back to Rachel's room.

He found her with her head on the pillow, eyes closed, shivering. He reached for the blanket on a table and carefully spread it out over her. When she felt the warmth, she opened her eyes again to see Brandon straightening it out to cover her legs. She gave him a small smile.

"How are you feeling?" he asked, brushing some hair off her forehead.

Rachel held her arm up a bit. "Considering I'm covered in my own blood and about to be sewn back together, I'm doing great." There was humor in her eyes, and Brandon chuckled.

"You're something else."

~

Rachel shut her eyes. Her arm was throbbing, but the pain in her head definitely trumped that.

Her next thought was about the stitches, and her stomach did a somersault. She'd never had stitches before, and imagining it made her anxious. She jumped a little when a woman wearing a colorful set of scrubs looked through the curtain, said hello, and wheeled in a cart. "Let's get your arm fixed up, shall we?"

She introduced herself and then began by cleaning the wound with a solution, something that was painful in itself. As she did, Rachel was surprised at how big the gash really was. Once the wound was clean, the nurse took out a syringe with a long needle. Rachel's stomach did another flip as she listened to the nurse explain how she was going to numb the skin a bit so she could stitch it together.

Brandon stepped closer to the bed, and Rachel felt herself relax a little.

As the woman gave her the shots, she made a point of watching the clock, her fist clenched involuntarily. Her eyes went to her hand when she felt Brandon touch it softly, uncurling her fist and taking her hand in his. She gave his a quick squeeze of thanks and went back to studying the clock.

It took some time to get the gash sewn closed. Rachel fell asleep shortly afterward, and it felt like only moments before the doctor had returned to do another exam.

"Good news! I'm clearing you to go home. We'll get you some instructions on how to care for that gash. You need to keep the laceration clean and change the dressing once a day. Try not to lift anything with that arm if you can help it. And like I said before," he turned his attention to Brandon, "this young woman needs to be awakened every three hours through the night." He patted Rachel's hand and smiled. "You were a very lucky lady."

Brandon got the paperwork together and signed her out of the hospital.

"Okay, it's time to get you home," Brandon told her, and Rachel wasn't about to argue. The doctor had given her something for the pain, and she was starting to feel pretty sleepy. She barely noticed Brandon helping her with her seat belt after getting into Charles and Sarah's truck. "Is Kendra doing okay?"

Brandon nodded. "Trent brought a car seat here and they got her home. She's sleeping. I hope it's okay, but they offered to keep her at their house in case we were late and I told them that was fine. I can go and get her first thing in the morning."

"Is my car totaled?"

"Yeah, it's gone. After all the bad luck you've had with that car, it's probably just as well."

Rachel barely managed a smile before she laid her head against the door, welcoming the sleep that claimed her.

~

Rachel woke up, vaguely able to recollect Brandon awakening her several times through the night. She turned her head to look at the clock on the side table, seeing that it was already nine in the morning. She tried to shift her weight and groaned. It was then that she saw Brandon sitting in the chair nearby. It looked like he'd been asleep, but when he heard her moving, he came forward to sit on the edge of the bed.

Brandon looked concerned. "How do you feel this morning?"

"I kind of hurt all over." Rachel winced as she struggled to a sitting position. She looked down to see she was still in the clothing from the night before. "How about you?"

"My neck and back are pretty sore, too. Mom texted me and said that Kendra is acting herself this morning so I think she must be okay. Praise God."

"Yes, praise God. It could have been so much worse."

~

Rachel managed to take it easy for several days

after the accident and avoided painkillers — something she was insistent about since they had made her feel so woozy the night of the accident. Brandon took a few days off to stay with her to help with Kendra. Sarah brought a pot of soup for them for dinner, and Melinda promised to send something over the following day so Rachel wouldn't have to mess with cooking for a bit.

By the end of the fourth day, Rachel was feeling mostly herself and had convinced everyone that she could return to work the following morning. She was ready to get back to normal. Before heading to bed, she went to the bathroom to change the dressing over her wound. Brandon had helped her wrap her arm back up each evening, but at this point, she was starting to feel like a pro. Rachel set out the supplies on the counter and tried to find the edge of the tan, stretchy bandage so she could start unwrapping it. She jumped when she saw the reflection of Brandon watching her in the mirror. "Hi," she said softly.

"Hey. Let me help with that." Without waiting for permission, he took over where she left off, removing the rest of the bandage and laying it on the counter. Next, he took the tape off the gauze that was piled on top of the wound. "I'm going to go slow, tell me if this hurts."

Carefully, he began to peel the gauze away from her arm, going slowly in case it was sticking to any of her skin — an issue that had presented itself the first couple of times the bandage had been changed. Brandon watched her face to make sure she wasn't in any pain. When she looked at him, their gazes locked until Rachel dipped her chin. She could feel her heart pounding and hoped Brandon wasn't able to hear it.

Brandon lifted the last piece of gauze, exposing the long, red cut. There was bruising all along it to match the bruising on her head, all of which were slowly moving from dark purple to shades of yellow and green. She was feeling a bit like a rainbow, but at least it was proof that her injuries were healing. The seven stitches made the laceration look worse in a way.

"Let's clean this up." He reached for the antibacterial wash and moved her so that the arm was over the sink. Slowly, he poured the solution over the wound, and she braced against the pain. "I'm sorry," he said with a cringe. But Rachel didn't make a sound as he cleaned the wound and placed a fresh piece of gauze over it. After the tape, he wrapped it again with the bandage and secured it. "Too tight?"

"No, I think that's fine. Thank you."

"No problem." He paused, touching the bruise on her head lightly then withdrawing his hand.

Rachel closed her eyes. When she opened her them again, she found him watching her in the mirror. She drew in a shaky breath.

Brandon slowly turned her to face him. Rachel felt her heart pounding as he ran a finger down her cheek and then slipped it under her chin. Lifting it gently, he touched his lips to hers for a moment, pulling away again.

Before Rachel could analyze or think about what happened, Brandon was kissing her again. Rachel leaned into him as he deepened their connection, his strong arms surrounding her. After a few moments he broke the kiss, touching her lips with his thumb. "You'd better get some sleep." With that, he walked out of the bathroom, leaving Rachel to stare after him.

Chapter Twelve

"I kissed her." Brandon looked at his brother as they loaded more buckets of apples.

Trent glanced up from what he was doing and raised an eyebrow. "Did she kiss you back?"

"Well, she didn't object."

Trent chuckled. "I guess that's a good sign."

"I keep trying to figure out what to do next. Any suggestions?" Brandon waited, but his brother said nothing. "A lot of help you are," he said good-naturedly.

"Keep doing what you're doing, Brand," Trent told him. "You've got to have faith. God's led you both this far. He's not going to bring you to this point and then let you both just walk off the edge of a cliff."

"It shouldn't be this hard." Brandon regarded him seriously. "I'm officially impressed that you and Dad found a woman for life."

Trent burst out laughing, and after his attempt to remain serious failed, Brandon joined him.

~

"I have a surprise for you," Brandon said as Rachel was getting dinner on the table.

Rachel looked at him, her gaze curious. "Oh?"

Brandon held his hand out and opened it, a cell phone cradled in his palm. "I bought it for you today. I programmed everyone's numbers in there for you."

Rachel wasn't sure what to think about the gesture. "You didn't need to do that, Brandon. I'm fine without a cell phone. And I know your number by heart."

"You do?" Brandon sounded surprised.

Rachel recited the number and received an impressed nod.

"I would still like for you to take it with you in case you ever need it. It would have been handy when your car stalled in the rain," he pointed out.

Rachel nodded and smiled. "Yes, it would have." She reached out and took the phone from him. "It was very thoughtful. Thank you, Brandon."

"You're welcome." Brandon beamed at her.

~

That evening, Brandon went upstairs to help Rachel with her bandage again. He felt as though there was an elephant sitting in the room with them. Neither of them had commented on their kiss the night before. He removed the gauze to clean the gash. It was healing so well, he had no doubt she should be able to have the stitches removed at her appointment. "How's it feeling?"

"It's sore after working today. But it was good to

155

actually do something again, so it was worth it. I do appreciate your help with this. Every time I see it again, I'm so thankful that no one was seriously hurt."

Brandon studied her for a moment. "I know you believe that life is just floating around on the ocean going from one storm to the other. I remembered one of my favorite songs the other day and thought it might mean something to you." He held a hand out to her. "Will you come down to the den, and I'll play it for you?"

Rachel looked surprised. "Sure."

They walked downstairs together. Brandon went to his CD player and put a disc in, choosing the correct track. "It's a song performed by Scott Krippayne called 'Sometimes He Calms the Storm.' Listen to the words, Rachel. I completely believe this is true, and it helps me when I feel like I'm working through a problem and God is nowhere to be seen."

Rachel sat on the couch, listening intently as the music swirled around them. It immediately struck a chord with her, but it wasn't until the chorus began that she felt as though the song were written for her. Tears sprang to her eyes as the song described how God will sometimes command the storm to end, while other times, He instead chooses to gather His child close as the waves threaten to overwhelm.

By the time the song was over, Rachel was in tears. Brandon sat down on the couch next to her and put an arm around her shoulder. "Sweetheart, God doesn't always rescue you from the situation you're in. Instead, He gathers you into His arms, and helps you to weather the storm. If you can remember that, you can cling to Him instead of trying to brave the storm yourself. You're never alone."

Rachel buried her face in his chest, and he pulled her close as she cried — really cried. He wondered when she last allowed herself to mourn and to open her heart. As she sobbed, he prayed for her, prayed that God would heal her emotional wounds with a balm so complete that she would feel relief from the pain she'd been carrying for so long. He prayed that she would let God into her life — into her heart — so that He could guide her and comfort her. Brandon also prayed that he could be a source of strength for her.

He said nothing as she cried, simply stroked her hair softly and held her. Gradually, the tears eased and she took a deep breath. He reached for a tissue from the coffee table and handed it to her.

Rachel took it from him and sat up straight, blowing her nose and wiping her eyes. "I'm sorry. I'm sure you didn't need me crying all over your shirt like that."

Brandon shook his head. "When was the last time you let yourself feel like that?" he asked.

Rachel sniffed. "Truthfully? I don't remember."

"Then you have nothing to feel sorry for, it was something that was long overdue. Besides," he looked down and pointed to the wet spots on his shirt, "you're welcome to cry on my shirt anytime you need to. I think it's a good look for me."

That brought a laugh, and he smiled back at her. "That's better!" Brandon used a finger to collect stray hairs that had gotten in her face and deposited them behind her ear. "You should probably go get some sleep and rest your arm before I start getting sappy on you."

Rachel looked at him, seemed to think about what

he said, and decided to heed his advice. "Goodnight, Brandon."

"Goodnight, Rachel."

~

Brandon was shocked Sunday morning when he looked up to find Rachel in a stunning turquoise blouse and new khakis.

Kendra stepped forward, modeling her own new pants and a purple shirt. "What do you think? Isn't it pretty?"

"You look beautiful," Brandon told her, scooping her up into his arms in a hug. "You are the two most beautiful ladies I know!" That brought a giggle out of Kendra

Rachel curtsied graciously, her cheeks flushing. "Do you mind if we come to church with you this morning?"

Mind? Brandon wouldn't have told her no for the world. "Of course not — you're always welcome."

When Brandon walked into the church building with Kendra in his arms and Rachel by his side, he felt like the luckiest man on the planet. Once they got Kendra set up in the preschool room, he led Rachel into the main church area and they took a seat a few rows away from his parents. With a wave, they settled in for service.

As heads bowed in prayer after the service, Brandon reached for Rachel's hand, holding it gently in his own. *Father, please help us both. Lead us down the path You want us to take. Protect both of our hearts and leave our minds open to possibilities — whatever those possibilities might be. Amen.*

When the prayer was over and everyone stood to gather their things, Brandon lifted Rachel's hand to his lips and kissed the top of it before squeezing and letting it go. Then he bent over to retrieve his Bible. Brandon caught her eyes and gave her a smile before moving so she could exit the row in front of him. He couldn't get over how right it felt to have her there at church with him.

~

Rachel was peeling and chopping another apple — she'd lost count hours ago. Kendra and Benjamin were playing in the living room. Sarah and Melinda were chatting and she hadn't meant to, but she was tuning them out.

The truth was, her mind was swarming with thoughts of the church service the day before, the song lyrics that Brandon had played for her, and the coming court date. She would be lying if she said memories of their kiss wasn't making an appearance on a regular basis, too.

Things had changed a lot in the last few days, and Rachel was struggling to keep up with the transitions. If someone asked her how she felt about any one of those things, she wouldn't have known what to say.

The next court date was approaching fast. Less than three weeks away. What if the judge awarded custody of Kendra to her great-aunt and uncle? The thought of never seeing that little girl made her feel as though someone was holding her underwater, and she had to shake her head to clear the emotions that overwhelmed her.

Suddenly something occurred to her that never

had before. What if the Lawrences were afraid of the same thing — afraid of losing the last link to their nephew? Thinking about that stilled her hands. She must've been standing there, doing nothing, for a while because both Sarah and Melinda had walked up to her, clearly concerned.

Sarah touched her shoulder and Rachel started. "Do you need to take a break?"

Rachel shrugged. She chopped another couple of apple slices and then stopped again. "I've been so worried about the Lawrences taking Kendra away from me, I only just realized that is exactly what I'm trying to do to them, too." She looked up. "Is it wrong of me to take Kendra away from two members of her own blood family?" Melinda and Sarah stayed silent. And really, what were they supposed to say? Rachel sighed and returned her focus to the apples.

~

Brandon was worried about how quiet Rachel was at dinner. He tried to draw her out in conversation, but she only offered him yes or no answers. When dinner was over, she left to get Kendra ready for bed. He was getting worried that she wasn't going to come back downstairs when he heard her bare feet step off the bottom stair and into the hall. When she entered the living room, he set the book he was reading aside and gave her his full attention. "Do you want to talk about it?"

"How am I any better than Kendra's great-uncle and aunt?"

"What do you mean?"

"I'm so worried about them taking Kendra away

from me. It's been overwhelming this week. Yet, what if they feel the same way? Kendra is the last link they have to Ryan. And I'm trying to rip that away from them."

Her words surprised him. She'd been so focused on what she had to do to keep Kendra — so had he — that he hadn't stopped to consider the other side of the coin, either. "Are you reconsidering fighting for custody?"

"Not at all. Even if all of my emotions were left out of the equation, logistically I'm the best person to take care of Kendra. But alienating her from the Lawrences — I can't see how that is a good thing."

Brandon nodded. "I hadn't thought about it like that, but you're right. They probably do feel the same way that you do. So what are you thinking?"

"Your mom mentioned that you all usually celebrate Thanksgiving with a nice dinner. That's a little over a week away." Rachel chewed on the edge of a fingernail. "I would want to ask your parents first. What if I invited the Lawrences to join us for dinner? They would have a chance to spend some time with Kendra. What if I showed them that they were welcome to be a part of Kendra's life?"

Brandon marveled at the changes he was seeing in Rachel. If someone had suggested this a couple of weeks ago, she would have resisted. "Are you sure that's something you want to pursue?"

"The truth is, if they'd gotten custody of Kendra, and if they offered me an olive branch like that, I would jump at it. I would feel so very grateful to get to spend a holiday with my niece instead of being shut out of her life." Rachel's voice broke. "I think this is something I need to do."

Brandon couldn't help the smile that came to his face. "I think that's a great idea. It can't hurt. Worst case, it ends badly and you won't hesitate to continue with your original plans."

Rachel lifted an eyebrow at him. "I sure don't want to ruin the holiday for your family. That wouldn't be fair. Nothing like arguments and a fistfight to bring the Thanksgiving spirit to the table."

Brandon laughed loudly at that. "But it would make it a memorable one." He gave her a hug, resting his chin on the top of her head. He was incredibly thankful for what God was doing for his wife, and the changes that were coming into her heart. "You can ask my mom. But as far as they're concerned, you're family and they'll be happy to invite the Lawrences to join us for Thanksgiving." He used his arms to set her apart from him a bit so he could see her face. She hesitated, but the sparkle in her eyes told him that she was happy with the decision. He thought the fact she was willing to risk something like this was a good sign. Maybe she was starting to have a little faith in the kindness of other people.

~

Having the stitches removed was a whole lot less painful than when they were originally placed — a fact that Rachel was especially thankful for. The doctor told her that she would have to keep the wound clean and it would probably take a couple of weeks to heal completely but, other than the scar, there shouldn't be any lasting effects.

The next morning, she was surprised by how much easier it was to get dressed when she wasn't worried about tearing any stitches. Kendra woke up in a giggly mood. Rachel tickled her under the chin, and Kendra collapsed to the floor in laughter. "Now I'm gonna tickle YOU!" She leapt up and went after Rachel with hands formed like claws.

Rachel feigned fear and ran from Kendra, allowing the girl to catch her as she tried to go through the door. They were both still laughing when Rachel chased her downstairs for breakfast. She had arranged with Sarah to arrive for work a little late that morning because she wanted to call Ryan's aunt and uncle. She wanted some privacy to do that. To say she was nervous about the phone conversation was an understatement.

Mrs. Lawrence's confused voice prompted Rachel to introduce herself, feeling awkward. Of course, the older woman knew who she was, but sounded surprised.

"Why have you called, Rachel?" Mrs. Lawrence asked her.

Rachel cleared her throat. "Look, I know this is going to sound strange. I also know how much Ryan meant to you and it didn't seem right for you not to spend the holiday with his daughter. With Kendra." She paused, clearing her throat again. "I was wondering if you would like to join us all for Thanksgiving dinner."

There was silence, and it lasted long enough that Rachel was starting to wonder if the line had gone dead. She thought she heard the other woman sniff before she said quietly, "We appreciate the invitation. Thank you. Let me check with my husband tonight and get back with you. Will tomorrow be early enough?"

Rachel assured her that it would be fine and gave the woman her new cell phone number. There was a huge sense of relief when she ended the call, placing her phone in her back pocket, and then walked with Kendra to Sarah's house.

~

Brandon's students filed out of the classroom. It was Friday, and he was very much looking forward to having the following week off for Thanksgiving. It would be a full week to spend with his family. All of his family, including the two newest members. He refused to acknowledge the possibility that this coming holiday may be the only one he got to spend with them.

It was less than two weeks until the court date. He felt his heart constrict as he imagined a clock ticking the time away. "God, I realize none of this is in my control. Please, give me the strength. Give Rachel and I the wisdom to know what we're supposed to do. And ultimately, let Your will be done."

That last part was said with some effort. Brandon knew what he wanted to happen if it was all up to him. But he tried to remind himself that only God had the finished picture. Only God knew how all the pieces of the puzzle of his life fit together to create the image God had in mind for him. He did find comfort in that.

He had some loose ends to tie up at the university, and it was nearly five before he even got to leave campus. By the time he walked through the front door of his home, his stomach was rumbling. The smell of fried chicken immediately filled his nostrils.

Brandon found Rachel and Kendra in the dining room. Kendra was sitting at the table, a roll in her hand, as she tore little bits of it off. When she saw him, her face broke into a huge smile. "Hi, Brandon!"

"Hi, munchkin!" Brandon gave her a hug. "Something smells good in here!"

Rachel was getting plates out of the cabinet when she turned and offered him a smile. "Just in time. Have a seat."

He tossed his messenger bag to the floor next to a table leg. Before sitting, he took the plates from Rachel and set them down on the table then got silverware while Rachel got them both something to drink. They sat across from each other as they had gotten accustomed to with Kendra at the end between them. Rachel made sure Kendra had what she needed before turning to her own meal.

Brandon offered her the plate of fried chicken and then took several pieces for himself.

They chatted about their day while they ate. Brandon enjoyed listening to Kendra's stories about how Candy helped can applesauce and how it was the best applesauce she or Candy had ever tasted.

"Will you have much work to do during the break?" Rachel asked him.

Brandon swallowed his bite. "I have some organizational stuff to do. I'll do that this weekend and then won't have to worry about anything next week."

They were silent for a few minutes. Brandon jutted his chin toward the phone. "Did you hear back from Mrs. Lawrence?"

Rachel nodded. "Yes, she called this afternoon. They accepted the invitation."

Brandon studied her a moment. "Is that good or bad?" he asked, because he couldn't quite read the emotion in her eyes.

"It's good. I know it's crazy, but I'm already nervous." She held a roll in her hand but didn't take a bite. "It's the right thing to do. I hope your parents don't regret agreeing to it," she added with a chuckle.

With a laugh, Brandon shook his head. "They won't regret it. But I will be praying all week. For them. And for you. That God would give you the wisdom and the words you need while they're here."

Rachel seemed to consider what he said, tilting her head slightly. "I appreciate that." Her attention turned back to the little girl who had slowed down with her food and was rubbing her eyes. "I think someone is getting sleepy," she said.

Kendra tried to protest but rubbed her eyes again and yawned.

Brandon smiled fondly at the little girl. When he looked back at Rachel, he found her watching him. He gave her a wink, which caused pink to color her cheeks. She stood to clear the table.

He cleared his throat. "I wondered if you and Kendra might have a picnic with me by the pond one day this week." He watched her back as she paused.

"That would be fun."

Before allowing himself to change his mind, Brandon stepped in front of her and smiled warmly into your eyes. "I'm looking forward to it." He brushed her lips lightly with his own. "Dinner was great. Thank you." He smiled again and left the room.

Chapter Thirteen

The weekend and Monday went by quickly — too quickly for Brandon's liking. But he chose to focus on the picnic planned with his family that Tuesday instead of the court date that was fast approaching. He knew Rachel was putting together the lunch, but he had stopped by a store and picked up some double chocolate chip cookies to take with them. Since Kendra loved chocolate so much, he was pretty sure they would bring a smile to her face.

When they were ready, he got Kendra's umbrella stroller and waited for the ladies outside. Kendra was so excited, she insisted on walking, but both of the adults knew that she was going to want to ride in the stroller on the way back home.

Brandon liked how easy it was for them to converse and joke back and forth as they slowly made their way to the pond. Rachel seemed completely at ease, and Brandon was loving it.

Kendra spotted a butterfly and stopped in her tracks. "Oh, Mommy, look!" In a moment, her smile fell away, and she looked up at Rachel, her face strained. "I meant Auntie." Kendra looked down at her shiny black shoes that didn't at all go with the pair of jean overalls she was wearing. "I'm sorry," she whispered, her voice tortured.

Tears immediately sprang to Rachel's eyes as she looked down at her niece. Brandon watched as she knelt down and drew the girl into her arms. "My sweet, sweet baby. Please don't feel bad." Rachel sat right down on the path, and Kendra curled up in her lap. "Your mommy and daddy loved you so much. And do you want to know something?" Kendra nodded slightly. "They are looking down right now from heaven, and they're smiling. They're smiling because they're so very proud of how brave you are and how sweet you are." Brandon felt moisture gather in his own eyes as he watched Rachel take Kendra's face gently in both of her hands. "I am so incredibly proud of you, too. You make me happy each and every day." She kissed her and then held her close again.

"I miss them," Kendra whispered.

"Me too, sweetheart." Tears trickled down Rachel's cheeks as she laid one of them against Kendra's hair. "It will keep getting better, I promise. As long as we keep hugging each other, it'll get better."

It took all he had for Brandon to not go down and pick both of his girls up and hug them. Instead he prayed for them, lifting their hurts to God.

When they were ready, Brandon helped them stand back up. He gave them a hug together. "You are a couple of amazing gals, did you know that?" Kendra nodded while Brandon and Rachel shared an amused grin.

Kendra scrambled down to explore some more as they continued walking to the pond. Brandon reached for Rachel's hand, marveling at how perfectly it fit into his. He noted how soft her skin was as he used his thumb to lightly rub the top of hers.

The lake was beautiful. Brandon spread a blanket out on the grass, and Kendra immediately began to gather small, yellow flowers and piled them on one corner. "You can't have a picnic without lots and lots of pretty flowers!" she declared. Rachel laughed, filled a small bowl with water from the pond, and showed her how to arrange the flowers in there so that they would last longer. Kendra was thrilled because the bowl was so big that it meant room for more flowers.

The cold fried chicken, macaroni salad, applesauce, and cookies all tasted even better outside in the beautiful weather. It was still plenty warm enough, but there was no doubt that this was one of the last pleasant afternoons before fall morphed into winter.

After eating, Kendra went back to collecting flowers and rocks, though it wasn't long before she had curled on the blanket next to Rachel and fell asleep. "She was awake with nightmares again last night," Rachel explained.

Brandon nodded and reached over to smooth the girl's hair back. It was clear she was going to be asleep for a while. He looked at Rachel, weighing his words. "You know it's very possible that she may want to call you mom one day."

Rachel took a deep breath but didn't respond. Brandon was about to change the subject when she finally said in a whisper, "I have so many mixed feelings about that." She looked up to meet his eyes, her own pools of confusion. "She deserves to grow up with a mom. I want to be that for her. But at the same time, I feel like letting her call me that is like forgetting all about Macy."

Brandon put an arm around her shoulders and hugged her to him. "Now that isn't true at all. Are you planning to tell her all about her parents as she grows up? Are you planning on telling her the funny and embarrassing stories about things that Macy did? Are you going to remind her how much she looks like her mom?" Rachel nodded against his chest. "Then you aren't going to let her — or yourself — forget about Macy. In fact, you're going to keep her alive for Kendra who is going to go forward and do the very same thing."

Rachel sniffed, and Brandon placed a kiss to her temple.

"Women become mothers in many different ways." Brandon wished he'd had the chance to meet Rachel's sister. He had a feeling the sisters were a lot alike. Though he hadn't told Rachel, he also thought Kendra looked like she could be Rachel's own daughter, not just her niece. "Rae, I didn't know Macy. But if she was anything like you, I think she would want Kendra to call you mom and she would be happy to know she's being cared for and loved."

~

Rachel looked up at the clock for the tenth time that hour before returning her attention to the apple crisp she was making. She'd already placed the chopped apples and water mixed with cinnamon in the bottom of the pan. Now she was adding the butter, flour, and sugar combination in crumbles on the top. Finally, she sprinkled more cinnamon for good measure. The dessert had always been one of Macy's favorites, and making it now helped Rachel feel closer to her sister. Rachel had already made cranberry sauce and that was in the fridge cooling. A fruit salad was next. Sarah had insisted on handling the turkey, gravy, and stuffing while Melinda volunteered to bring the rolls and mashed potatoes. The Lawrences were also supposed to bring something to add to the dessert choices.

Just thinking about the Lawrences made her feel as though her stomach were threatening mutiny.

When everything was ready and it was time to get dressed, she changed into a pair of dark jeans and a maroon, long-sleeved shirt. She brushed her hair out, taking a tiny bit on one side and braiding it, bringing it back over the top of her head to the other side like a headband.

Kendra had insisted on wearing a dress — a pretty purple one with white lace on the cuffs. Brandon had surprised her with it the previous day. That he had remembered the dress when Rachel admired it at the mall warmed her heart. In a rare nod of agreement, Kendra allowed her to pull part of the girl's hair back and secure it with a purple ribbon. "Baby girl, you look like a little princess!" she exclaimed, the smile on her face matched with one of Kendra's own.

"So do you! We look like two princesses!"

Rachel laughed and picked the girl up, dancing with her as she sung one of Kendra's favorite Disney movie songs. Brandon walked in and joined them, dancing together with Kendra in the middle. "I couldn't let you two have all of the fun!"

They had only been at Charles and Sarah's house

twenty minutes before there was a knock at the front door. She looked at Brandon, who gave her a smile of encouragement before he joined her in answering the door.

Steven and Jennifer Lawrence stood at the entrance, looking about as uncertain as Rachel was feeling. She made herself smile as normally as she could. "Hi! We're so glad you could make it. Please come in." Rachel stepped aside and motioned for them to enter.

Mrs. Lawrence had two pie pans in her arms that she held almost like a shield. She glanced at her husband. "Thank you for the invitation."

Brandon stretched a hand out to Mr. Lawrence, who hesitated a moment before sharing in a hearty handshake. "Let me take your coats."

By now, the other members of the family had trickled out to meet the guests. Rachel made the introductions as Sarah offered to take the pies and put them in the kitchen. Kendra and Benjamin ran into the room and Kendra stopped, looking at the newcomers.

Rachel knelt next to Kendra. "Sweetheart, this is your great-uncle Steven and great-aunt Jennifer. They are your Daddy's aunt and uncle."

Kendra looked up at them, eyes wide. "Hi," she said shyly with a small wave as she leaned into Rachel's shoulder.

Mrs. Lawrence approached her, limping slightly, and smiled. "You can call me Aunt Jen. And it's very nice to see you. We only saw you when you were a tiny baby, and I wish we could have visited with you more often."

Mr. Lawrence joined his wife. "And you can call

me Uncle Steve." He cleared his throat, his voice heavy with emotion. Hearing that, Rachel looked over at Mrs. Lawrence and could see the moisture in her eyes. It was then that Rachel knew, in her heart, that inviting them was the right thing to do.

It was time for Thanksgiving dinner, and Brandon reached over to capture Rachel's hand as they headed for the dining room. "You did a good thing here," he whispered to her. "I'm proud of you." He placed a kiss to her cheek near her ear. "Let's go stuff ourselves with food."

Rachel giggled and allowed him to lead her to join the others.

Dinner was a success. By the time it was over and people were on their way out, everyone had become relaxed and even the Lawrences seemed to enjoy their evening. They also enjoyed interacting with Kendra who, after a couple of reminders, was more than happy to call them by the names they had told her. Rachel didn't miss the looks of peace and pleasure they both expressed upon hearing the little girl say their names.

Rachel walked the older couple out to their car, crossing her arms against the cool breeze and light rain that had begun to fall. Mr. Lawrence opened the door for his wife, but before she entered, she turned to Rachel. "Thank you so much for inviting us to be a part of tonight. It has meant more than we can say."

Mr. Lawrence gave her a nod in agreement. Rachel smiled, placing a hand on the woman's arm. "I'm truly glad you could come. I would like for us all to get together for Christmas, too."

The couple agreed enthusiastically. Before they could get too wet, they got settled in their car. With a wave, Rachel watched them disappear around the bend. The evening had been perfect — so much better than she had thought it would be. She looked up toward the sky. "Thank you," she whispered, and then turned to go inside.

~

Brandon waited in the kitchen for Rachel to return after tucking Kendra in bed. The girl had been so tired that they had to work together to keep her awake on the short drive home. Brandon welcomed Rachel with a smile and a glass of cold water. She accepted the water gratefully and took a seat at the table. "That was the best Thanksgiving meal I've ever had," she said. "Your mom outdid herself."

"So did you. Your apple crisp is a new favorite. I hope you know it'll be requested again before next Thanksgiving." He raised an eyebrow in mock seriousness and that made Rachel laugh.

Brandon wished he could read her mind for one night, to see what was going on in her head. It felt like months since they had been horseback riding, and he'd felt hope for their future together. It also felt like months since he'd kissed her, and he was starting to wonder if it was all just a dream.

With the court date approaching fast, he knew she was overwhelmed and nervous. The last thing he wanted to do was pressure her or take advantage of emotions that were already charged. So he pushed down the almost overwhelming desire to pull her into his arms.

"I definitely need to thank your parents for allowing me to invite the Lawrences," Rachel was saying. "It was a great evening, wasn't it?"

She looked at him, her eyes glittering with happiness. He nodded. "Yeah, it was."

"Thank you, too, Brandon. You kept me sane tonight."

Rachel's words surprised him. "I think you underestimate yourself, Rae. You had it all under control."

She shook her head emphatically, raven black hair coming over her shoulders and brushing her arms. She paused, as though she were trying to find the right words. "There are very few people in my life that I would consider a friend." She looked at him, her eyes serious. "You are one of them."

Brandon knew immediately what she meant. While he may feel much more than that for her, he had to agree. Even if the situation were different, and she had still been his student, he thought they would have developed a friendship. "I feel the same way, Rachel. I'm incredibly thankful for you and the role you play in my life."

Brandon could feel his heart racing, could feel the pulse in his throat. He wondered if Rachel could hear it, too, or if she was as affected by this evening as he was. He held her gaze for a while before she broke it, setting her glass down on the counter. "I guess we should get some sleep," she said. Was that disappointment in her voice?

Before she could skirt around the island and head out of the room, he moved to step in front of her. When she raised her eyes to his, he could see what he felt sure mirrored in his own gaze. He immediately pulled her into a hug, relishing the feel of her wrapped in his arms. "Never hesitate to tell me if you need a hug — because chances are, I do, too," he whispered into her hair. He felt her nod against his chest, praying for this woman even after she had stepped back and gone upstairs to bed.

~

"I can't help but feel like I'm running out of time," Brandon explained to Trent as he helped his brother chop firewood. He wiped sweat off his brow with the arm of his long-sleeved shirt that was only a shade lighter than the blue sky above them. "A week-and-a-half until the court date. Why do I feel like my life is either going to end or begin on that date, too?"

"Because you're human." Trent drove the head of his ax into the stump he was using to chop wood on and took a swig of water. "And you're completely in love with a woman with whom you don't know where you stand."

Brandon thought about that and agreed. His brother was right. He wasn't falling in love with Rachel. He had fallen a while ago and had landed hard. "I feel like I should lay it all out in black and white for her. But do I do that before the hearing? Or after?"

Trent blew air out, thought a moment and shrugged. "I don't know that either one is perfect timing."

Brandon swung his ax and split another piece of wood into two, further reducing it into a total of four. The fact was, he was afraid of the answer. If he bared his heart and she didn't feel the same, it was the end. At least right now he had hope. And wood to chop, which was at least helping him reduce his frustration one swing at a time.

~

Rachel watched as Melinda's hand went to her abdomen. The baby was moving so much that even Rachel could see the rippled effects underneath the maternity shirt. "If this baby's personality in utero is anything like it will be when he or she gets here, you may have your hands full," Rachel commented.

Melinda's eyes widened as she laughed. "You're not joking." She motioned toward the two kids playing. "Or it could be the opposite, like Benny. He was calm and very scheduled with his awake times before he was born. Now look at him. Our miniature tornado."

It was Rachel's turn to giggle. When she looked over, she found Melinda watching her. "Do you want to have kids, Rachel?"

"Yeah, I do." Rachel was fully aware of how wistful her voice sounded, and it surprised even her. "I always have. I figured I would adopt at least one or two so they wouldn't have to go through what I did. But I always hoped I would be able to have at least one of my own, too."

"It's worth it." Melinda patted her belly. "Every burp, uncomfortable position, and sleepless night. It's worth it all."

Rachel laughed again and found herself staring out the window as white clouds began to roll in and conceal the deep blue of the sky.

"Love is a choice, you know." Melinda's words brought Rachel's attention right to her. "If you feel like you could fall for a certain brother-in-law of mine, then choose to let it happen." Rachel's face must have registered the shock she felt because Melinda held up a hand. "I'm sorry. It's none of my business." She seemed to consider just how much she should say. "God brings so many blessings our way. Sometimes they're obvious enough you would have to be blind to miss them. And other times, they're so subtle that if you blink, they could be gone. But either way, it's up to us to choose to embrace those blessings and bring them into our lives."

"No, don't apologize." Rachel felt like her mind was racing a mile a minute. "I appreciate your honesty. I had never thought about it like that before — love being a choice. A lot of the time I feel like I don't have a choice over most things in my life."

"That's a tactic Satan is using against you. He knows that you're vulnerable to that, and he'll use it as long as you give him the power to do so." Melinda gave her a smile that was filled with kindness and understanding. "This situation you and Brandon are in is a unique one. But if you take everything out of the equation except for how you feel about Brandon, what does your heart tell you?"

Melinda's words caused Rachel to raise an eyebrow, her mind buzzing. She returned her gaze to the window. If Macy hadn't died, if she wasn't trying to raise Kendra on her own, and if she had gotten to know Brandon, her instructor, like she knew him now... She was reluctant to go there but her heart immediately told her the truth. Realizing she had been staring at nothing, she turned her attention back to the woman across from her. "Melinda, everything is still part of the equation."

The other woman's smile was understanding.

"And despite that, you feel the same." It was a statement, not a question.

Rachel pinched the top of her nose between her thumb and forefinger, letting out a sigh. "A choice, huh?"

Chapter Fourteen

Kendra's screams woke Rachel with a start. She jumped out of bed and hurried across the hall. The little girl was thrashing back and forth in her bed, still asleep. Rachel sat down and scooped Kendra onto her lap. "Shhhhh. It's just a dream, sweetheart. Open your eyes." She smoothed her niece's hair out of her eyes. "Look at me, Kendra."

The girl's eyelids fluttered, and she seemed to focus on Rachel's face. "There we go. See, you're safe. Everything is okay." Rachel kissed her forehead and tried to wipe some of the sweat off of her face and neck as she hummed softly. With Rachel rocking her, it didn't take long for Kendra to fall back to sleep.

Rachel placed her back in bed. "There we go, my girl," she whispered. "You have sweet dreams the rest of tonight." With a light kiss, she left the room and closed the door again behind her. She found Brandon standing in the hallway.

"Is she okay?"

"Yeah, she's fine. She's already asleep again."

"I'm glad." Brandon nodded toward her door. "It

seems like she's getting easier to calm down."

Rachel agreed, a peaceful smile lighting her face. "Yes. The nightmares are becoming less frequent, too. I think her heart is on the mend." As she said it, she knew that it was true — not just for Kendra, but for herself as well.

~

Rachel rose early Saturday morning. After checking on Kendra, she quietly padded through the house and out onto the front porch. It had been raining all night, and it looked like it wasn't going to let up anytime soon. Pulling the light jacket she was wearing tighter around her, Rachel leaned her arms on the railing. She listened to the sound of the raindrops as they hit the roof that covered the porch.

Puddles had coalesced in the grass. As additional raindrops hit the puddles, they formed ripples that collided with each other. Rachel inhaled deeply.

The front door opened, and Rachel turned her head to see Brandon joining her. "Good morning," she greeted, moving to face the yard again.

"Good morning." Brandon stepped behind her, wrapping his arms around her. "You warm enough?"

She nodded with an, "Mhmmm." Rachel let herself lean into his solid frame, soaking in his warmth and strength. "Does the university teach any photography classes?"

"Yes, they have several of them. I've heard the instructor, Professor Walsh, is quite good. Why is that?"

"I need a hobby, and I thought I might like to try my hand at photography." Rachel motioned to the puddles. "I was watching the rain fall and thinking about how beautiful the puddles looked with all the designs the ripples were creating. I was wishing I could capture it somehow."

Brandon released Rachel and moved to stand next to her, his back against the railing so that he could see her. "I think that's a great idea." When she looked at him, she found his gaze full of approval. "You can chronicle Kendra's childhood that way, too."

Rachel nodded. "That's what I was thinking."

"It would be nice to have you back on campus." Brandon said and Rachel chuckled. He pointed a finger at her. "I still miss having you in my class. You were the highlight of my day."

"Even before all of this started?"

"Oh yeah, even then." Brandon raised an eyebrow.

Rachel felt her face grow warm. "At that time, I had no idea."

"I know, that's part of your charm." He winked at her, effectively deepening the red in her cheeks. She couldn't help her grin. "You're impossible to ignore, Rae." Brandon reached over and took her hand in his. "You are special — in so many ways. You deserve to have someone show you that every day of your life."

Rachel focused on the feel of her hand in his much larger one. He'd told her how he felt and yet here she was, hesitant to voice what was in her heart. She remembered Melinda's words about Satan using her fears against her. Rachel felt as though a great deal of her life had been governed with fear. She was tired. Tired of worrying about everything all the time. Tired of wondering when the next shoe was going to drop. Tired of handling it all on her own.

~

Brandon gave Rachel's hand a slight squeeze, hoping to encourage her to open up with what was weighing so heavily on her. "Sweetheart, talk to me."

"I've been feeling more and more at peace about the court date. I think everything is going to work out."

Brandon marveled at how the worry that had seemed to etch itself on her face had slowly disappeared over the last few days.

Rachel turned to fully face him, her hand still in his. "Whatever happens with Kendra, I..." she paused, took a deep breath. "I need you, Brandon."

Brandon reached for her, pulling Rachel to his chest in a hug. "I need you, too." He kissed the top of her head. "I love you, Rachel." He pulled back enough to study her face. "I love you, and I can't imagine my life without you and Kendra in it."

Brandon searched Rachel's eyes. He found they mirrored his own as Rachel replied with a quiet, "I love you, too."

The couple smiled at each other in wonder as the rain continued to fall, now going completely unnoticed. Brandon cupped her face with his hands. He placed kisses to her forehead, the tip of her nose, and then finally claimed her lips in a kiss that was sweeter than any he could have imagined. He pulled back, his eyes caressing her face. "You are an answer to prayer, girl."

Rachel reached up and gently fingered the hair at the nape of his neck. "I feel like God has been showing me that I need to let go and trust. Trust Him. Trust you." She took a deep breath. "I feel like

I'm finally home."

Brandon captured her lips again, tugging her closer and letting his fingers bury themselves in her hair.

~

The first day of December was gloomy as low clouds hung in the sky with the promise of rain in the near future. It seemed like it should be much later since the clouds were blocking the sun's light. Rachel had to remind herself that it was Monday. She knew Brandon had to go into work early to get some stuff prepared on campus, but she was still disappointed to see he was already gone when she awoke.

Downstairs, she found a note that he had left on the fridge telling her that he couldn't wait to come home and see her that evening. It was the "Love, Brandon" at the end that caused Rachel to smile and made her heart feel as though it were singing.

"Come on, Kendra, let's get some breakfast. What do you want to eat?"

"Pancakes!" Kendra was hopping up and down, clapping her hands.

Rachel laughed at the girl's enthusiasm. "I think I can do that. Why don't you go play in the den for a few minutes while I mix some up?"

"But I want to help you, Auntie."

"In that case, drag that chair over here, and you can pour in the milk."

Rachel had just finished the pancakes and set one drowning in butter and syrup in front of Kendra when her cell phone rang. She glanced at the clock to see it read nine on the dot as she answered the phone. "Hello?"

"This is Mary O'Dell. I'm calling about the custody case between you and the Lawrences."

Well, Rachel hadn't expected that. "Good morning. What can I help you with?"

"I've spoken with the Lawrences at length. They have agreed to drop the custody battle on one condition."

Rachel wasn't even sure she'd heard that right. "Condition?"

"That they be allowed to see Kendra, keep in touch with her, and be a part of her life."

Rachel felt moisture gather in her eyes and had to blink fast to clear her vision. "I don't think that will be a problem."

"Fantastic. We are going to keep the original court date, but it will be used to read the agreement and finalize everything."

"Thank you." Rachel hung up and laid the phone down on the counter.

"Is something wrong?" Kendra asked from her spot at the table.

Rachel smiled at her, her heart feeling lighter than she ever thought possible. "My dear, sweet girl. Nothing is wrong in this world." She picked her niece up from the chair and swung her around the room. "God answers prayers, and don't you let anyone tell you differently."

Kendra's smile was brilliant as she laughed at her aunt's antics. "Auntie, I love it when you dance with me."

"I love it when you dance with me, too," Rachel told her before giving her a giant bear hug.

~

The court hearing went smoothly. It was agreed that the Lawrences would be involved in Kendra's life. Rachel told them that family was something she had lacked as a child but that she wanted Kendra to be surrounded by as much family as possible. She and Jennifer Lawrence hugged as tears were shed.

Rachel and Brandon were officially named Kendra's permanent legal guardians. Rachel felt as though Macy and Ryan were smiling down on them, happy to know that so many people loved and cared for their daughter.

That evening, Rachel was standing in the doorway to Kendra's room as she watched the girl rock Candy before laying her down on a bed of towels that she had gathered for the toy monkey's nap. Rachel heard footsteps, and soon Brandon's strong arms were circling around her. She leaned into him with a sigh of contentment.

"Life is good," he said simply, nuzzling her ear before kissing it.

Rachel nodded. "You want to hear something amazing?" She could feel Brandon nod. "During the court hearing, I kept thinking about how much loss Kendra has gone through and how I — or all of us, really — were there to hold her, comfort her, and help her get through it." Her voice caught and she cleared her throat. "Out of nowhere, I swear something reminded me that is exactly what God had done for me my whole life. If He hadn't been there to hold me and help me through the bad times, I'm not sure I could have made it."

Brandon gently turned her in his arms so that he could see her face. His smile was both filled with understanding and love. "I'm sorry you had so many challenges, but it made you who you are and it brought you to this point in your life." He kissed her softly. "I love you just the way you are."

Rachel relished the feel of his closeness.

Kendra ran at them, throwing herself at their legs. "Make room for me!"

The adults laughed as they picked her up and held her between them. "We always have room for you." Rachel's gaze flitted from Kendra to Brandon. "I love my family."

Kendra's little hand grasped Rachel's.

"We love you, too, Auntie."

Rachel's Apple Crisp Recipe

4 cups sliced apples
¼ cup water
1 tsp. cinnamon
1 cup sugar
¾ cup flour
1/3 cup soft butter

- Preheat the oven to 350°F
- Spread the sliced apples in the bottom of an ungreased 8" x 8" pan
- Combine the water and cinnamon in a bowl and then sprinkle that over the apples
- Work sugar, flour, and soft butter together until it is crumbly
- Spread the mixture over the apples evenly
- Sprinkle more cinnamon on top of the mixture according to your preference
- Bake uncovered for approximately 40 minutes

Acknowledgments

I can't even express how excited I am to be writing this. There are so many people who played a part in the journey that led me here. Without you, *Calming the Storm* would not have come together.

I want to give a heartfelt thank you to:

My wonderful husband, Doug. You have encouraged me, challenged me and you never let me give up on my dream. I am so blessed to call you my best friend, soulmate, and husband. I love and appreciate you!

Our amazing kids, Xander and Sydney. You have both been so patient with me through this whole process. You are my inspiration every day. I love you, X-Man and Sydney Bug!

My parents, Bob and Suzanne Allison; and my brothers, Matthew Allison and Michael Allison. I would not be who I am today if it weren't for each of you. I love you all!

Howard and Amy Shults, my wonderful grandparents. You read every story I sent to you as a child and still have many of them. Thank you for always being there for me. Much love to you both!

My sweet friend, Amanda Knox. I am so blessed to call you my sister and my friend. You are the first person to have read this book in its entirety. I so appreciate your feedback, ideas, and the laughter we share. Love ya, girl!

My talented editor, Kristen Tribe. You sacrificed so much time to go through my manuscript with a fine-toothed comb. I appreciate your help in making this book something I am proud to share with everyone.

Susette Williams, my mentor. You have been a huge help to me as I've navigated these uncharted waters. I appreciate your time, your experience and your friendship.

The wonderful people who read this book, gave me your feedback, helped with ideas for the cover and so much more. Doug Snitker, Suzanne Allison, Matthew Allison and Kim Smith. Your opinions and advice were invaluable.

My Lord Jesus Christ. I owe everything to you and I am so incredibly blessed with the life you have given me. My life is a wonderful adventure and you are my guide. Whether you calm the storm or hold me close as I weather it, your love never fails. May this book be for your glory.

About the Author

Melanie Snitker is the author of the Love's Compass series. She has enjoyed writing fiction for as long as she can remember. She started out writing episodes of cartoon shows that she wanted to see as a child and her love of writing grew from there.

She and her husband live in Texas with their two children who keep their lives full of adventure, and two dogs who add a dash of mischief to the family dynamics.

In her spare time, Melanie enjoys photography, reading, crochet, baking, archery, camping and hanging out with family and friends.

Books by Melanie D. Snitker

Calming the Storm
(A Marriage of Convenience)

Love's Compass Series:

Finding Peace (Book 1)

Finding Hope (Book 2)

Finding Courage (Book 3)

Finding Faith (Book 4)

Life Unexpected Series:

Safe In His Arms (Book 1)

Made in the USA
Monee, IL
08 December 2020

51279437R00108